"Guess that answers

"So we know the bellows ma[...]
but"—Louis's voice rose in [...]
dry-wash doing here and who [...] it. It
wasn't here yesterday."

"Yes, it was." Squatting, Ray pointed to the
ground where the imprint of the old machine was
still visible in the gritty soil. "We just didn't see
it. *Yesterday* it was lying on its side and the rocks
blocked our view."

"Okay, Dad." Planting his hands on his hips,
Louis grinned at his father. "You set this thing
up and rigged it to run, right? So we'd believe in
Grandpa's ghost."

Mr. Driscoll shook his head. "No, Louis. I didn't."

"I don't see any footprints." Nicole stepped forward to study the nearby terrain, then gasped.

She pointed to a spot several feet on the far side
of the dry-wash.

Alex's throat went dry when she saw the following
words scrawled in the dirt:

GET OUT!

The Secret World of Alex Mack™

Available from MINSTREL Books

NICKELODEON®

the secret world of

ALEX MACK™

Gold Rush Fever!

Diana G. Gallagher

A MINSTREL® BOOK

Published by POCKET BOOKS
New York   London   Toronto   Sydney   Tokyo   Singapore

A MINSTREL PAPERBACK *Original*

 A Minstrel Book published by
POCKET BOOKS, a division of Simon & Schuster Inc.
1230 Avenue of the Americas, New York, NY 10020

ISBN: 0-671-00703-3

First Minstrel Books printing August 1998

10 9 8 7 6 5 4 3 2 1

Cover photography by Stacie Turk and Danny Feld

Printed in the U.S.A.

For Benjamin Heller,
who has an adventurous spirit
and a heart of gold

Gold Rush Fever!

CHAPTER 1

"I thought we were only going to the desert for the weekend, Louis." Alex Mack stared at the huge pile of duffel bags and camping gear in the Driscoll driveway.

"Yeah!" Robyn Russo dropped her wide-brimmed straw hat on top of her backpack and sleeping bag.

Louis shrugged. "Well, my dad likes to be prepared."

"Looks like he's ready for anything." Raising an eyebrow, Nicole Wilson picked up a heavy lined jacket. "Including snow in August."

"I packed a sweater just in case," Ray Alva-

1

rado said. "The temperature can drop forty degrees on the desert after the sun goes down."

"I've got a sweater *and* a turtleneck." Alex grinned. They had been planning the weekend expedition to go dry-wash gold mining with Louis and Mr. Driscoll for a week. She had packed according to the warnings and hints Louis had dropped about conditions on the Driscoll claim, which was located in a vast region of desert wilderness three hours north of Paradise Valley. Although there could be drastic differences in the temperature between day and night, the desert sun was hot. She had bought a khaki-colored canvas Australian bush hat just for the trip. Although one side was turned up and pinned to the crown, the front brim would protect her from heat exhaustion. Which, Alex thought, might be a bigger problem than she had realized.

"The weather report said it was going up to a hundred and ten degrees on the desert tomorrow." Nicole tossed the jacket back onto Louis's pile. "I think we'll be lucky if the temperature plunges into the *nineties* after sundown."

"It's going to be *that* hot? I'll melt!" Dismayed, Robyn sighed with resignation.

The discussion was cut short when Big Lou Driscoll pulled up to the curb in a large four-wheel–drive utility vehicle, pulling a compact tent trailer. Alex wondered where Louis's father planned to stow their gear and still have room for them, too. The truck's cargo bay was already stuffed with camping gear and gold mining equipment. A long, rectangular panel was attached to the carrier rack on the roof.

Alex smiled as Louis's dad leaped out of the all-terrain truck and waved. Tall and trim with a receding hairline, Mr. Driscoll was not only fascinated by the weird gadgets he developed and sold, he was a salesman with a knack for showmanship. As Louis liked to point out, his dad could sell earmuffs to people who lived on tropical islands and suntan lotion to residents of the far north in the dark of Arctic winter.

"Everybody's here, I see!" Clapping his hands together, Mr. Driscoll beamed. "Ready for the adventure of a lifetime?"

Robyn grimaced. "Digging buckets of dirt under a broiling sun isn't *exactly* my definition of an adventure, but I'm ready."

"So am I." Ray's eyes sparkled with anticipation. "I just hope we actually *find* gold."

"We'll find gold." Louis grinned. "But we'll work hard for it. Most of the time the ratio of gold found to dirt dug is about one speck of gold in a billion specks of dirt."

"We know, Louis," Alex said. "You've told us that at least a dozen times since you invited us to go."

"Then again," Louis added mischievously, "we might hit a huge deposit that's full of gold nuggets."

"That's what makes looking for gold so exciting!" Mr. Driscoll exclaimed as he picked up two sleeping bags. "You don't know what you're gonna find."

"All the scorpions and rattlesnakes we disturb will probably find *me!*" Robyn shuddered.

"That's a definite possibility, Robyn." Louis nodded. "Just hope that you don't get bitten by one of those little copper-green scorpions. They're the worst! Mojave green rattlers aren't exactly a picnic, either."

"Don't worry, Robyn," Mr. Driscoll said. "We always carry an antivenin kit."

Seeing how quickly the blood drained from Robyn's face, Ray jumped in. "But you've never had to use it, right?"

"Nope," Mr. Driscoll said. "Never have."

Nicole frowned. "I'm just not sure I like the idea of digging holes in the ground to look for gold. I mean, major mining operations are responsible for irreparable ecological destruction all over the world."

Rolling his eyes, Louis tugged on the handle of a large cooler filled with ice and sodas. "The damage we can do in a weekend won't matter on a global scale, Nicole."

"And coming home with some gold would be so totally cool." Reaching for her duffel bag, Alex paused to stare wistfully into space.

Robyn sighed. "The only thing I'll get is a sunburn."

"And an aching back from digging," Nicole teased.

"It'll be fun." Alex slung her bag over her shoulder. "And kind of like going on an adventure *back* in time."

"Very true, Alex." Mr. Driscoll looked back as he reached the tent trailer. "We'll be using the same methods the old prospectors did a hundred and fifty years ago during the California Gold Rush. With a few modern improvements."

Alex started slightly. "But Louis said your

equipment was designed and built just like the pioneers'."

"Basically. The operating principles of the dry-wash and panning methods are the same. I've just added a few inventive touches of my own." Mr. Driscoll pointed toward the rectangular panel on the utility vehicle. "Like using solar power to generate electricity to run the motor connected to the dry-wash. The pioneers used hand-powered bellows to classify the ore."

"Huh?"

Noting Alex's blank stare, Mr. Driscoll smiled. "I'll explain everything tomorrow when we set up."

Ray grabbed the other handle of the large cooler and helped Louis tote it to the curb. "Have you, uh . . . tested these improvements yet, Mr. Driscoll?"

Alex blinked, sharing Ray's concern. Mr. Driscoll's gadgets didn't always work the way they were supposed to. His battery-operated back scrubbers didn't operate when they got wet. No-slip work gloves stuck to rake and shovel handles—permanently. And Driscoll carbonated beverage bottle stoppers turned into mini-rockets that launched explosively at temperatures below sixty degrees, a design flaw that had caused numerous dings and dents inside refrigerators throughout Paradise Valley.

"Sure have, Ray." Mr. Driscoll frowned thoughtfully as he triggered the mechanism to open the tent. "And *this* time, I'm pretty sure I've got all the bugs worked out."

Setting the cooler down, Louis shook his head.

Ray nodded with a tight smile as he dropped his end.

Alex exchanged skeptical glances with Robyn and Nicole. Fortunately, Mr. Driscoll didn't seem to notice their lack of confidence regarding his inventive prowess.

"Okay, gang! Let's get the rest of this gear stowed and hit the road." Mr. Driscoll checked his watch. "By my calculations, we should arrive in plenty of time to set up camp before the sun sets."

Alex smiled with genuine enthusiasm. It really didn't matter if they found gold or if Mr. Driscoll's inventions botched the whole gold mining process. It had been a while since they had spent time simply enjoying each other's company. Everyone was eager to leave the midsummer boredom and the routine of home behind for a couple of carefree days in the desert.

Sandwiched between Ray and Louis in the backseat of the utility vehicle, Alex watched the landscape change from cultivated green to desert brown while Mr. Driscoll entertained them with stories about the California Gold Rush. It had started in the winter of 1848 during the construction of Sutter's Mill, when one of the workers had found a gold nugget in the American River channel.

"John Sutter owned fifty thousand acres in the Sacramento River valley and he begged his workers to keep the discovery a secret."

"He wanted to keep all that gold for himself, right?" Nicole asked.

"Actually, no," Mr. Driscoll explained. "Sutter wanted to build a trading empire. If word about the gold got out, he knew his land would be invaded by hordes of people crazed by gold fever, which would ruin his plans. It was a good thing they managed to keep it a secret for a while, too."

"Why?" Ray asked.

"Because the Mexican-American war was

going on and California wasn't part of the United States yet," Mr. Driscoll explained. "Mexico gave the California territory to the United States in the treaty that ended the war—nine days *after* gold was discovered at Sutter's Mill."

"And no way Mexico would have done *that* if they had known about the gold," Robyn added.

"You've got that right." Louis grinned. "But even though the news traveled only by word of mouth back then, it didn't take long before it *wasn't* a secret anymore."

"Not long at all." Mr. Driscoll shook his head. "One month after the news hit San Francisco, three-quarters of the men had left to look for gold. Soldiers deserted camps and sailors jumped ship. Merchants left their stores and farmers left their fields. Even the teacher in the town's only school locked the doors and took his students to the gold digs."

Louis nodded. "And it wasn't long before people were pouring into California from all over the world."

Robyn sighed. "I can almost picture this massive wave of miners with picks and shovels flooding in."

"Yep. There was an epidemic of gold fever."

Mr. Driscoll smiled. "I remember reading a quote by someone who had caught it. He said, 'A frenzy seized my soul.' "

Ray shrugged. "Well, I can understand why. I mean, maybe a lot of those guys didn't have much to leave behind."

"Very true, Ray," Mr. Driscoll agreed. "There was a famine in Ireland and most of Europe was at war. Not to mention that some of the gold miners were making three hundred dollars a *day* and soldiers and sailors were only paid six or seven dollars a month."

"Seven dollars a *month?*" Ray sat back. "Well, I would have packed up and gone west, too."

"Exactly," Mr. Driscoll said. "Besides, gold fever is highly contagious."

"I've got a natural immunity to greed," Nicole joked.

"*Nobody's* immune to gold fever." Louis grinned. "You'll be digging right along with the rest of us, Nicole."

"I wouldn't bet on that," Nicole said.

"We'll see." Louis smiled. "When someone spots that golden sparkle on black sand for the first time, the fever hits hard. Believe, me. I know."

Everyone fell silent as Mr. Driscoll slowed the truck to match the speed limit through a small town.

Alex noted a sign declaring that the population of Red Mountain was one hundred and thirty. The town was as bleak and brown as the endless miles of barren desert and rocky bluffs surrounding it. With a small café, an ancient service station, a general store, and a scattering of run-down houses and shacks, Red Mountain looked like it was only a heartbeat away from becoming a ghost town.

"So how did you happen to end up owning a gold claim, Mr. Driscoll?" Ray asked as they hit the open highway again.

"Well, actually, I don't own it yet. My father has the rights to the Rabbit River claim."

"Rabbit River?" Robyn eyed Mr. Driscoll curiously. "There's a river there?"

"There was a hundred years ago," Mr. Driscoll clarified. "It's just a dry riverbed now."

"But there *is* a river of rabbits!" Louis chuckled. "The place is overrun with them."

"Rabbits I can deal with." Robyn grimaced. "It's the snakes and scorpions that give me the creeps."

"Don't forget the coyotes," Louis teased.

Ray was still focused on the idea of owning a gold mining claim. "But the rights to the claim will go to you someday, won't they?"

Mr. Driscoll nodded. "Sooner than I expected, actually. My father has had the Rabbit River for thirty years. He used to come up three or four times every summer to get out of the city and work it."

"He came all the way from Cincinnati?" Ray asked.

"No!" Mr. Driscoll laughed. "I took a job in Ohio right after Louis's mother and I were married, but I grew up in California. Gold mining was one of my dad's hobbies."

"Correction. It was a way of life for Grandpa." Lowering his voice to sound gruff, Louis mimicked his grandfather's voice. "Diggin' for gold toughens the flab, fuels the heart, and eases a weary mind like nothin' else *knooown* to man!"

"What do you mean, '*was* one of his hobbies,' Mr. Driscoll?" Alex asked cautiously.

"He retired out of state last spring and can't work the claim anymore," Mr. Driscoll said. "Which is why Louis and I *had* to get up here this weekend!"

"Had to?" Ray frowned, confused.

Louis nodded. "If we want to keep the Rabbit River."

"My dad is going to sign the claim over to me," Mr. Driscoll explained, "but he'll lose it if we don't take care of the government's assessment requirements. The annual maintenance fee is due soon."

"How much is it, Mr. Driscoll?" Ray flinched when Alex nudged him in the ribs. "I'm just curious, Alex."

"It's no secret!" Mr. Driscoll laughed. "The same rules apply to everyone who owns a claim. I either have to make a hundred dollars' worth of improvements, do a hundred dollars' worth of work—or pay a hundred dollars."

"But it's a Driscoll family tradition to do the work," Louis added. "And with six of us working, we won't have any trouble satisfying the government's regulations."

Robyn blinked at Mr. Driscoll, then looked back to her friends. "Is that why you were so anxious for all of us to come, Louis?"

"To work so you wouldn't lose your claim?" Ray arched a questioning eyebrow.

"No!" Louis laughed nervously, then shrugged. "All right. That *was* part of it."

"What's the other part?" Nicole asked bluntly.

Mr. Driscoll scowled at Louis in the rearview mirror. "You told me your friends wanted to come and help out."

"We do!" Alex quickly interjected. "We just didn't know it was so important."

"Okay." Holding up his hands, Louis confessed. "So I didn't want to be stuck up here with my dad's friends all weekend. No offense, Dad, but you old guys can get pretty boring."

"Point taken, Louis," Mr. Driscoll said calmly, "but that's no excuse for misleading your friends."

"Yeah," Ray said.

Alex held back a smile. Ray wasn't upset. He was just getting a charge out of giving Louis a hard time.

"I wasn't trying to pull a fast one, Ray. I just thought that if you knew keeping our claim depended on how much work we did, it would spoil the fun of looking for gold."

"I think the fun will be *finding* gold!" Ray said.

"We will." Louis grinned. "My grandpa's got jars full of gold dust, gold flakes, and even some pretty good-size nuggets. And it all came out of the Rabbit River claim."

"Jars full?" Robyn's eyes widened.

"It took Dad thirty years to find that much, but . . ." Mr. Driscoll paused for dramatic effect, "he's sure a rich vein runs through our claim. We just haven't found it yet."

"I'm glad we can help you out, Mr. Driscoll," Alex said. "I think it would be a shame to lose a gold claim that's been in your family for thirty years."

Ray was in total agreement. "Especially a claim that's actually *got* gold."

Mr. Driscoll hesitated, then nodded solemnly. "Not to mention a notorious ghost."

CHAPTER 2

"Give it up, guys." Settling back against the seat, Louis smiled. "Dad's not going to tell you about the ghost until later. And *I've* been sworn to secrecy."

"Yep!" Mr. Driscoll chuckled. "Ghost stories should always be told around a campfire. In the dark. Besides, we're almost there and we've got a lot of work to do setting up camp."

Alex grinned as Mr. Driscoll turned off the two-lane highway onto a rutted dirt track. Nothing they said had been able to prod him into talking about the ghost, but trying had helped pass the time.

"But—there's nothing here!" Robyn exclaimed.

That's not quite true, Alex thought as she studied the bleak panorama. Miles of bleached dirt and brown rock stretched toward the mountains that pierced the distant horizon to the right. The desert wasn't really empty, Alex mused as the road wound into the hills and gullies on the left. The harsh terrain evoked a sense of isolation that *felt* like nothing.

Scrubby bushes with greenish brown leaves struggled to survive in rocky clefts. Huge boulders perched on high ledges silently tracked the truck's passage. Other large rocks had fallen into depressions, victims of erosion, earthquakes, and gravity. Round, dried tumbleweeds rested against craggy inclines or rolled across the open spaces, driven by a brisk desert breeze. Grasses and wildflowers that had bloomed in a kaleidoscope of color after the spring rains had withered under the hot summer sun.

"What's that?" Ray pressed against Alex for a better view out the window as they rounded a bend in the road.

Alex stared at the ruins of a wooden shack by the side of a bluff. The wind had blown the shingles off the roof and there was no glass in the windows. The porch overhang sagged and the open door was hanging from a broken hinge. Rusted buckets, an overturned wheelbarrow, a shovel, and other junk was strewn across the yard. A hand-scrawled sign on a stake near the road read: KEEP OUT!

"That's the Rock Bottom claim," Mr. Driscoll said. "According to local legend, nobody's ever found a single flake of gold on it. It's a bad-luck dig and no one's tried to work it for over fifty years."

Alex sighed. The desert was *not* at their mercy as Nicole believed. The abandoned Rock Bottom claim was a harsh reminder that *they* were at the mercy of the elements.

"You were right, Alex," Robyn said. "This *is* sort of like going back in time."

"Or being in one of those old black and white western movies," Ray added.

"Yeah." Alex grinned. "I almost expect to see an old, bearded prospector walk out from behind the rocks with a burro and a pickax."

"That can be arranged," Louis quipped.

"Give me a break, Louis." Robyn's blue eyes flashed as she looked back over her seat. "Nobody prospects with a burro anymore."

"No, but Matt Montgomery has a pet burro. And a beard."

"Matt owns the Amanda Jane." Mr. Driscoll jerked the steering wheel hard to the right to avoid a deep rut. "The claim that borders ours."

Louis sighed. "There're dozens of claims with people living on them out here, but *we* had to get crazy old Matt for a neighbor."

"How crazy is he?" Robyn shifted nervously.

"He's not crazy at all." Mr. Driscoll shot Louis a warning look. "He's just a little eccentric."

Louis whispered in Alex's ear. "Old Man Montgomery is totally looney tunes."

Alex tensed. Between the mysterious ghost, the bleak isolation of the desert, and the Driscolls' eccentric neighbor, she couldn't help feeling a little uneasy.

"Old Matt is a loner," Mr. Driscoll went on. "We hardly ever see him and he rarely stops by to make small talk. All he does is dig—"

"There's the marker!" Louis pointed through the windshield at a short white wooden post in the ground. "Welcome to the Rabbit River claim."

"Too cool!" Ray grinned.

"Eureka!" Nicole laughed.

"Isn't that what we're supposed to say *after* we find gold?" Robyn teased.

"Totally awesome," Alex said.

Louis frowned thoughtfully. "No, I don't think anyone on the old frontier said 'totally awesome,' Alex."

Laughing, Alex cuffed Louis on the shoulder, then turned her attention back to the window as Mr. Driscoll drove up a slight incline.

The Rabbit River claim was on a higher elevation than the Rock Bottom. Mr. Driscoll explained that the claim ran a hundred yards into the steep face of the western cliff. The high butte cast a massive shadow over the land as the sun dipped lower in the sky. Most of the site consisted of dips and swells dotted with boulders and scrub bushes. The northern end was a long, gradual slope down to the dry riverbed that marked the boundary. Two hundred yards to the east, a sheer drop-off marked the boundary between the Rabbit River claim and the Amanda Jane below.

"Okay!" Parking on a level spot at the base of the high, rocky butte, Mr. Driscoll turned off the engine and faced the five kids. "Everybody out!

The sooner we get the camp set up, the sooner we eat."

No one needed a second invitation. However, after being in the air-conditioned truck for three hours, stepping out onto the desert was like stepping into a blast furnace.

Robyn staggered, wilting instantly. "It's after seven o'clock and it must still be a hundred degrees out here!"

"At least," Alex gasped. The breeze blowing through her hair felt like the hot breath of a huge invisible dragon.

"By midnight you'll be freezing, Robyn," Louis said.

"At midnight I'll be sound asleep in my very warm sleeping bag." A sudden gust of wind ripped Robyn's straw hat off her head. "My hat!"

"I'll get it!" Ray took off as the hat sailed eastward toward Matt Montgomery's claim.

"Don't go over the edge!" Louis called frantically as he raced after Ray. Robyn and Nicole ran close on his heels.

Alex realized they wouldn't catch the hat before it sailed over the drop-off. Grabbing it with a telekinetic thought, she pinned it to the ground and smiled. Once again, the powers she had acquired after being doused with the gene-altering compound GC-161, when a Paradise Valley Chemical truck almost hit her the first day of seventh grade, had saved the day. It was amazing how often being able to move things with her mind or zap electricity from her fingers or turn into a puddle came in handy.

Scooping up the hat, Ray skidded to a stop.

Louis scowled as he and the girls braked beside Ray on the ridge. "That was a lucky break, Robyn."

Ray smiled knowingly at Alex. He was the only one of her friends who knew her secret.

Taking back her hat, Robyn peered over the edge at the ground twenty feet below. "We could have gotten down there, Louis. It's not that steep."

"But down there is the Amanda Jane," Louis said. "Not the Rabbit River."

Alex was surprised to see a small camp trailer with a tattered awning on Matt Montgomery's site. A storage shed with a lean-to on one side had been constructed from oddly shaped pieces of plywood and rippled tin panels. The shed stood about thirty feet away from the trailer and an old army jeep was parked behind it. Buckets, wheelbarrows, tools, and assorted junk were scattered around the property. There were holes and mounds of dirt everywhere.

Louis fixed his baffled friends with a serious stare. "The people that live on their claims are pretty friendly—as long as nobody trespasses on their land."

"So people really do live out here?" Robyn asked, aghast. "All the time?"

Louis nodded. "Old Matt does. And Jenny and Bart Riley. They've got a big operation on the far side of the butte."

"What do they do about water?" Nicole asked curiously.

"Some of them truck it in. Like Matt." Louis pointed at a large water-storage container sitting on a scaffold made of sturdy corner posts with crossed rails for support. "The Rileys had to drill down six hundred feet before they hit water, but they've got a well."

"What's that weird-looking contraption?" Ray gestured toward a large bin that sat atop a smaller wooden support structure. Large piles of dirt had formed under a series of angled troughs that ran from the bin to the ground.

"That's just a bigger version of my dad's dry-wash." Louis stared at the large ore-processing apparatus for a moment before turning back to his curious friends. "There's one *really* important thing you all have to remember when we start working tomorrow, guys."

"What?" everyone asked in unison.

"Do *not* go past the posts that mark the corners of our claim. Friendly neighbors can turn real mean real fast if anyone even *touches* one of their rocks. Especially old Matt."

"You mean he'd get upset if we just wanted to get a hat back?" Alex asked.

"Feuds have started over less."

Nicole shook her head. "That is so ... mercenary."

"Maybe," Louis said. "But it's the law people live by out here."

"Just like the Old West!" Ray grinned.

As though to emphasize the point, a door slammed. Alex tensed as a scrawny man with a long gray beard and even longer gray hair paused outside the trailer door. Wearing a battered cowboy hat, a plaid shirt, baggy jeans, and boots, he looked liked the wizened, comical sidekicks all the old cowboy movie heroes used to have. Except Matt Montgomery wasn't amusing. His hard stare set Alex's nerves on edge.

A sudden, horrendous noise that sounded like the screech of a wheezing movie monster made everyone jump.

Robyn yelped. "What was that?"

"Beatrice." Smiling, Louis looked toward the lean-to. A small gray donkey walked out from under the sloped roof. "Matt's burro. Must be dinnertime."

The burro hee-hawed loudly again, trotted into the yard, and butted the old man with her muzzle, breaking the tension. Everyone grinned as Matt shooed the hungry burro away and headed for the shed. Following him, Beatrice kicked up her heels and sent a metal bucket flying into the air. Matt ducked to keep from being bucket–bombed.

"She's so cute!" Robyn squealed.

"I guess so." Louis shrugged. "Unless you happen to be on the business end of those hooves!"

"Hey! Let's go, gang!" Mr. Driscoll called. "The sun's going down!"

Fascinated by the burro, Alex paused to look

back as everyone else hurried toward the camp-site.

Ignoring Beatrice's insistent nudges, Matt turned to meet Alex's curious gaze with another hard stare. He pushed over a tin roofing panel that was propped against the shed as he turned to go inside.

Spotting the crude sign painted on the shed wall, Alex shivered as a gust of wind whipped past her.

KEEP OUT OR ELSE! THIS MEANS *YOU!*

Inhaling sharply, Alex froze.

She wasn't just startled by Matt Montgomery's scribbled warning.

The gust of desert wind had been icy cold, even though the air temperature still sizzled above ninety.

CHAPTER 3

"I think that's the best hot dog I ever ate." Patting his stomach, Ray leaned against a rock and closed his eyes with a contented smile.

"You mean the third one tasted better than the first two?" Alex pulled her sweater closed. The temperature *had* dropped after sundown and although the crackling campfire was cheerfully cozy, it didn't offset the chill.

Ray's only response was his smile.

"After three hot dogs, two helpings of potato salad, and chips, no wonder you can't move, Ray," Nicole teased.

"I ate *twice* as much as I usually do." Groaning, Robyn dumped her paper plate in the trash bag behind her. "If I'm not careful, I'll gain five pounds this weekend."

"I hardly think so, Robyn." Mr. Driscoll chuckled. "You'll work off those calories tomorrow."

"Yep. And you'll be starving by tomorrow night." Louis nodded, finishing off his hot dog bun. "I forget all about food when I'm digging."

Nicole started. "You forget about your stomach, Louis?"

"I find that hard to believe," Alex added.

"I know it's totally weird, but looking for gold has that affect on me. Guess I'd better eat as much as I can now." Reaching for his hot dog roasting stick, Louis grinned at his dad. "Where's the marshmallows?"

"Marshmallows?" Ray's eyes popped open and he sat bolt upright with his own stick primed and ready.

"Desert dessert." Opening a bag of the spongy white puffs, Mr. Driscoll handed it to Ray.

"Topped off with a ghost story?" Alex asked hopefully.

"I'm ready." Skewering a marshmallow, Ray

held his stick over the fire. "You can start any-time, Mr. Driscoll."

"It's not a totally gross story, is it?" Robyn asked.

"Strictly PG–13, Robyn." Leaning forward, Mr. Driscoll scanned their expectant faces. "But it's totally weird."

"I can do weird," Robyn said. "I just don't sleep well on gruesome."

Smothering a smile, Mr. Driscoll lowered his voice. "His name was Jack Rabbit Morgan. He lived and died on the banks of the Rabbit River over a hundred years ago, but they say he still roams this desert at night—"

Crunch! Crack!

Alex gasped at the sound of a snapping branch.

"What was that?" Robyn asked in a hushed rasp.

"An animal?" Ray shrugged.

Holding up his hand for silence, Mr. Driscoll glanced over his shoulder.

Crunch, crunch.

"Just don't tell me it's that Jack Rabbit guy," Robyn whispered.

"Ghosts don't crunch," Louis said.

"But *someone* is coming," Nicole hissed.

Peering into the darkness, Alex could just make out a shadowy form moving toward them. *Crunch.*

"Is that you, Matt?" Dr. Driscoll called.

"Yep." A hoarse voice answered back. Wearing an old denim jacket over his shirt, the old man stepped into the glow cast by the fire. "Just thought I'd check to make sure them kids wasn't *trespassing*, Big Lou."

"No," Mr. Driscoll said seriously. "They're here with me. But I do appreciate your concern."

Matt scowled. "You sure Ben don't mind you draggin' so many people out to his claim?"

"Quite sure, Matt. He'll be signing the claim over to me as soon as we've done the work to cover the assessment."

"Is that so?" A flicker of interest gleamed in the old man's eyes.

Alarm, Alex wondered, or simply a reflection of the blazing fire?

"Isn't it dangerous to be wandering around in the dark without a flashlight?" Nicole asked.

"I been livin' out here for thirty years, missy," Matt growled. "Ever since I claimed the Amanda Jane when the previous owner forfeited for not payin' his assessment. Right after Ben Driscoll got the Rabbit River claim the same way. Don't need no flashlight to find my way around these parts."

"And batteries are expensive." Louis glanced at the old man with a deadpan expression. "Right, Mr. Montgomery?"

"Yep." Scratching his bearded chin, Matt nodded. "I barely scrape enough gold out of the ground to get by. Don't need to waste my hard-earned money on conveniences."

Louis looked down in embarrassment from teasing the old man.

"Got time for a cup of coffee, Matt?" said Mr. Driscoll. "I was just starting to tell this crew about Jack Rabbit Morgan."

Matt perked up at the mention of the ghost. "Might as well. Don't have nothin' better to do in the dark."

Alex smiled as the old man sat down between her and Mr. Driscoll. Easing over to escape the odor of sweat and grime that tainted the air around him, she tensed when the old man eyed her narrowly. She hadn't meant to offend him.

The awkward moment passed when Mr. Driscoll handed Matt a mug of coffee poured from the camp pot resting on the edge of the fire.

"Want a marshmallow?" Ray offered the bag, but the old man ignored him.

Alex held out her stick.

"So git on with it, Lou," the old man said, gesturing impatiently. "I haven't heard anybody talk about Jack in a long while."

"Please do." Shivering, Robyn drew up her knees and wrapped her arms around them. "The real story can't possibly be worse than the ones I'm imagining."

"Don't know 'bout that." Matt grinned, revealing a mouth full of crooked teeth. "Jack's fate was pretty gruesome."

"More *mysterious*, actually," Mr. Driscoll quickly interjected when Robyn grimaced. "He disappeared."

"Like vanished into thin air?" Realizing her marshmallow was ablaze, Alex quickly withdrew it from the fire and blew out the flames.

"Just tell it from the beginning, Dad."

"In ghastly detail." Grinning, Alex popped the charred marshmallow into her mouth.

Nodding, Mr. Driscoll sipped his coffee. "Jack Rabbit Morgan staked and worked a claim somewhere along the river, when it was still flowing. That's a vital fact, 'cause you can't pan gold from dirt without water and it wasn't so easy to haul water back then."

"It's not that easy now," Matt mumbled.

Alex glanced back at the awning attached to the rear of the tent trailer. Four five-gallon water containers were visible in the glow of a lamp hanging from the awning frame. Mr. Driscoll had already told them that water was almost as precious as gold in the desert. He had brought more than enough for washing in a basin, panning, and drinking. Even so, they still had to conserve.

Mr. Driscoll smiled at Matt, then continued. "Now, you gotta understand that a *vein* of gold is gone once it's mined out of the rock. But that's not necessarily so when you're workin' the desert or a river. Geological forces push gold up to the surface on the desert and rivers carry gold that's been shaken loose by earthquakes downstream. As time passes, huge deposits can collect in certain locations."

"Is that why there's so much gold in California?" Alex asked curiously, remembering her sixth-grade history unit. "Because there are so many earthquakes?"

"Could be. The thing that's important to this story is that Jack Morgan had a really valuable claim. Not only was the river rich in gold, he also had plenty of water."

Nodding, Matt stared into the darkness with a pensive frown. "That claim might even have been the Rabbit River—or the Amanda Jane."

"Nobody knows exactly." Mr. Driscoll sighed. "Not many of the records from the early days survived."

Alex shifted her gaze between the old man and Mr. Driscoll, fascinated by the legend.

Ray's interest was a lot more immediate.

"You mean we could be sitting on top of a gold mine? I mean, a big one?"

Mr. Driscoll grinned. "My dad thinks so, Ray, but he never found a rich concentration. All the gold he took out of here he found one flake at a time."

"Bah. There's no big deposits around here." Matt waved away the idea with a gnarled hand. "These sites have been worked for over a century. All the big strikes were made a long time ago."

"Maybe. Maybe not," Mr. Driscoll said absently.

Seeing the sharp look old Matt gave Mr. Driscoll, Alex shifted uncomfortably. Lost in their own thoughts, no one else noticed. Even Nicole was strangely quiet, but Alex doubted she was thinking about the remote possibility of striking it rich. *She's probably brooding over all the environmental damage mining a large deposit would cause,* she thought with a smile.

"But what happened to Jack Rabbit Morgan?" Alex asked, breaking the prolonged silence.

Mr. Driscoll looked up. "Hmmm? Oh! The ghost."

"Please," Robyn pleaded. "Before my overactive imagination runs totally amok."

"Well, as the story goes, Jack caught two men changing his markers one night. They were burying marked rocks under his stakes so they could 'prove' the claim was theirs."

"Claim jumpers," Louis clarified, then yawned.

Alex glanced at Louis curiously. He looked bored. But then he had probably heard the story a hundred times. "The worst kind of crooks in the gold fields," Mr. Driscoll said. "When Jack surprised the two men, they jumped him! Jack fought bravely, but he was no match for two mean, gold-hungry thugs."

Nicole sighed. "So they did him in to get his gold."

"Not exactly. Jack managed to break free and escaped into the desert night." Mr. Driscoll paused, gazing into the darkness. "But he was never heard from again."

"So what makes people think he died and is haunting the claims now?" Ray asked, bewildered.

Louis grinned. "Because one of the guys that stole Jack Rabbit Morgan's claim lived to tell the tale."

"You mean one of them *didn't* survive?" Alex leaned forward intently.

"Yep." Mr. Driscoll poured himself another cup of coffee. "When Jack ran off, they heard him vow that *no one* would ever get the gold that was lawfully his. And that he would get rid of any claim jumper he caught on this desert. The man that survived abandoned the claim after his partner was killed in a mysterious rock slide."

"Creepy." Robyn shuddered.

"Yeah." Mr. Driscoll's eyes twinkled. "But personally, I think having a haunted claim is . . . totally awesome."

Alex grinned.

"More like totally dangerous," Matt said ominously. "So y'all better beware. 'Cause if this *is* Jack's old claim, he's not gonna let you take anything out of it."

"We didn't jump the claim," Louis reminded the old man.

Robyn frowned. "And your grandfather's got all those jars of gold—"

"What jars?" Louis interrupted, his eyes narrowed in warning.

Robyn blinked.

Mr. Driscoll glanced at Matt.

Crack!

The poles holding up the trailer awning collapsed, knocking over one of the water containers.

Everyone except Matt jumped up to save the precious fluid that was pouring onto the ground, but nobody succeeded.

Ray and Louis ran into each other and fell. Mr. Driscoll tripped over the soda cooler and sprawled on the ground. Robyn froze and Nicole's jacket caught on a branch.

Then the camp light blinked out.

Alex tried to push the fallen container upright using telekinesis, confident that no one could see in the dark. She gasped as a gust of icy cold wind swooped around her, making her stumble and disrupting her concentration. The container wobbled but only rolled over.

By the time everyone recovered and reached the tent, the water container was empty.

"I don't understand this." Running a hand through his hair, Mr. Driscoll sighed. "I'm sure the awning braces were secure and all the container caps were tight."

Strolling up behind them, Matt glanced at the pool of water as it seeped into the dry desert floor. "This sure looks like a warning from Jack Rabbit Morgan."

"Has anything like this happened before?" Ray asked.

Louis scowled. "Never. Not when I've been here, anyway."

Robyn and Nicole pressed closer to Mr. Driscoll.

Alex shivered. The air was chilly, but the wind

that had prevented her from saving the water had been freezing—and strong enough to throw her off balance. She couldn't shake the eerie feeling that Matt Montgomery might be right.

Maybe Jack Morgan *was* haunting the Rabbit River claim!

CHAPTER 4

Alex awoke feeling invigorated after falling asleep the instant her head hit the pillow. She had stayed in the tent with Robyn and Nicole, while Mr. Driscoll, Ray, and Louis had bedded down outside under the awning. They had all been too exhausted and unnerved to stay up talking. Considering she had dozed off wondering if a ghost had collapsed the awning, Alex was amazed she hadn't been plagued by nightmares.

"What time is it?" Nicole stretched on the opposite bunk. The middle section of the bunk could be raised up and converted into a table during the day. The ends remained in place, forming benches.

"Just after six." Turning away from the digital clock on the wall, Alex moved the canvas flap over the clear plastic window aside. Ray, Louis, and Mr. Driscoll were still alseep under the awning. In the eastern sky, the golden orb of the morning sun had just cleared the horizon.

Glancing at the sleeping form beside her, Nicole rigorously shook Robyn's shoulder. "Time to rise and shine, Robyn. Wake up."

Moaning, Robyn rolled over without opening her eyes.

"Don't bother, Nicole. It's hopeless." Alex sighed, remembering how hard it had been to roust Robyn out of bed when she had stayed with the Macks when her parents were in Europe. "She doesn't have to go to school or anything."

"Guess you're right." Taking a deep breath, Nicole slid off the bunk. "Funny, but I'm really hungry this morning."

"Me, too." Setting her bag on the bunk, Alex pulled out a clean set of clothes. "Must be the fresh air."

"Maybe." Nicole reached for her bag, then

hesitated. "Don't you think it's odd that Louis's grandfather keeps his jars of gold stashed here?"

"Oh, I don't know." Alex shrugged out of her rumpled shirt. Last night after Mr. Montgomery left, Louis had explained that Ben Driscoll kept most of his gold hidden on the claim. Louis obviously didn't want old Matt to know, just in case he couldn't resist looking for the stash after the Driscolls returned to Paradise Valley. "It's probably safer hidden out here than in his house in the city."

"Maybe." Nicole lowered her eyes as she started to change. "Or maybe he really believes in the ghost of Jack Rabbit Morgan and doesn't want to make him mad."

"Nicole! Are you saying you believe in ghosts?"

"No!" Nicole's eyes flashed defensively. "I'm saying that maybe Louis's *grandfather* does. And maybe he keeps the gold right here where he found it so Jack Morgan will leave him alone. That's all."

"I suppose that's possible," Alex said cautiously. "But Louis said that they've never had any trouble before."

"If I was Ben Driscoll, I wouldn't want my

grandson to know I was afraid of a ghost." Nicole's eyes narrowed thoughtfully. "And maybe they've never brought so many people up to dig here before, either."

Alex sighed. She had actually met the ghost of Danielle Atron's grandmother one Halloween, but that didn't mean the cold wind she had felt was Jack Morgan's ghost. There was probably a rational, scientific explanation for the chilling gust, even though no one else had felt it.

"But you know? The one thing we can't do without out here is water." Nicole slipped on her socks. "And that's what we lost last night. Water."

"And you think that means something important?"

"Yes! If we lost our water, Alex, we'd have to leave."

"I suppose," Alex conceded, but she wasn't convinced.

"And how do you explain the collapsing tent?" Nicole asked. "I *saw* Mr. Driscoll lock the braces in place and check the container caps to make sure they were tight."

"Obviously someone unlocked the braces and loosened the caps. But even though I think it would be super if there really was a ghost . . ." Alex shrugged. The idea of being harassed by a ghost did have a certain romantic appeal, but Alex was surprised by Nicole's determination to support the ghost theory rather than something more realistic. "Chances are Louis and Ray set that up to scare us."

"I hope so," Robyn mumbled. " 'Cause if there's really a ghost, I'm hiking out of here right now."

"Go back to sleep, Robyn." Nicole grinned sheepishly. "You're probably right, Alex. For all we know, it could have been Mr. Montgomery or one of the other—"

Whuff! Whuff! Whuff!

"Now what?" Squealing, Robyn sat up and clutched her sleeping bag to her chest.

Nicole and Alex both grabbed their boots and bolted for the door. The boys and Mr. Driscoll were getting to their feet as the girls flew out of the tent.

"What was that?" Ray rubbed the sleep from his eyes.

"I don't know," Louis huffed indignantly, "but I really didn't need an alarm clock this morning."

"Okay!" Sticking her head out the tent door, Robyn scowled. "This isn't funny, you guys."

"*We* didn't do anything!" Louis sighed.

Alex and Nicole exchanged anxious glances as they put on their boots.

"But I think the noise came from over there." Mr. Driscoll pointed to the ridge by the drop-off into the Amanda Jane. "Come on. Let's have a look."

Shading her eyes from the sun as she walked, Alex peered at the spot. She could just make out a wooden contraption that was almost invisible because the weathered wood blended so perfectly with the surrounding rock and sand. She didn't remember seeing it there when they had chased Robyn's hat.

"Wait for me!" Still wearing the wrinkled clothes she had slept in, Robyn raced to catch up.

"What is it?" Nicole asked as everyone stopped to stare at the crude device.

Alex glanced down at the Amanda Jane, but there was no sign of Mr. Montgomery.

Sighing, Mr. Driscoll scratched his head. "It's an antique version of a dry-wash."

Alex studied the old machine curiously, awed by a relic that connected the present to the past.

It stood about three and a half feet high on three legs. The fourth leg was broken, causing the dry-wash to tilt to one side. A torn canvas bag hung under a slanted wooden tray. Another rotting, wooden tray above the slanted tray was filled with dirt and rocks.

Reaching down, Mr. Driscoll gently grabbed two wooden handles attached to the canvas bag and pushed them together.

Whuff! Whuff!

"Guess that answers that question."

"So we know the bellows made that noise, Dad, but"—Louis's voice rose in pitch—"what's this dry-wash doing here and who was running it? It wasn't here yesterday."

"Yes, it was." Squatting, Ray pointed to the ground where the imprint of the old machine was still visible in the gritty soil. "We just didn't see it. *Yesterday* it was lying on its side and the rocks blocked our view."

"Okay, Dad." Planting his hands on his hips, Louis grinned at his father. "You set this thing up and rigged it to run, right? So we'd believe in Grandpa's ghost."

Mr. Driscoll shook his head. "No, Louis. I didn't."

"I don't see any footprints." Nicole stepped forward to study the nearby terrain, then gasped.

"What?" Startled, Ray looked up.

Stunned, Nicole pointed to a spot several feet on the far side of the dry-wash.

Alex's throat went dry when she saw the following words scrawled in the dirt:

GET OUT!

"That does it." Lifting her chin, Robyn did an about-face. "I'm leaving."

"I don't think so, Robyn," Louis said. "It's fifty miles back to the nearest town."

"Oh." Turning abruptly, Robyn came back. "Great. I'm stuck on the desert with a ghost who's got a grudge."

"Let's not jump to any unlikely conclusions just yet." Mr. Driscoll smiled reassuringly. "Old Matt's been trying to talk Louis's grandpa into giving up the Rabbit River for thirty years. So *he* can file a claim on it. He just might be trying to scare me off."

Catching Alex's amused glance, Nicole shrugged.

"Except old Matt can't fly."

47

"What's that supposed to mean, Louis?" Robyn asked.

Scanning the ground between the dry-wash and the scrawled warning, Louis went to the edge of the drop-off and looked down. "That old guy couldn't have gotten down this cliff and back to his trailer without us seeing him. Not in the two minutes it took us to get over here."

Ray sat back on his heels. "But that air-thing couldn't have *whuffed* unless someone was working it."

"Exactly," Louis said. "Someone who doesn't leave footprints."

"For the record, I am *not* having fun." Robyn wrapped her arms around herself and shuddered, even though the temperature had already risen past eighty.

"I'm sure Matt brushed out his prints." Mr. Driscoll started to move past the dry-wash to get a closer look at the ground. His advance was interrupted by a low roar.

Turning in the direction of the eerie sound, Alex gawked. A whirling, funnel-shaped dust devil carrying branches and debris was charging up the northern slope headed straight for them.

Mr. Driscoll paled and shouted, "Take cover!"

CHAPTER 5

Louis, Ray, and Mr. Driscoll hit the dirt and covered their heads with their arms. Alex, Nicole, and Robyn ran for a nearby pile of rocks and ducked behind it just as the desert tornado barreled across the rise.

Gripping the rough edges of the rock, Alex watched the swirling funnel rip bits of torn canvas and rotted wood off the old dry-wash.

The powerful wind missed the boys, but struck Mr. Driscoll so hard, it rolled him over. Then it skated along the edge of the ridge for several feet before doubling back to send small pebbles and dirt scattering on the ground and flying through the air.

Alex ducked as the dust devil roared past the rocks where she, Robyn, and Nicole were huddled. Gritty sand pelted her arms and the wind whipped her hair into a hopeless tangle.

And then it was gone.

Hesitating for a few seconds to be sure, Alex finally looked up, then crept out from behind the rocks.

"All clear!" Rising, Mr. Driscoll brushed the dirt off his jeans.

"Well." Smiling tightly, Nicole carefully pulled a tumbleweed twig covered with sharp, barbed seeds off her jeans. "That was extremely so exciting."

"Way too exciting, if you ask me." Wincing, Robyn scowled at a tear in her shirt and the scraped elbow underneath it. "I hope we have a first-aid kit."

Nicole glanced at the red scratches. "I think you'll live, Robyn."

Hauling themselves to their feet, Louis and Ray went to inspect the old dry-wash, which the dust devil had dragged closer to the brink of the drop-off. A wooden leg had been severed and the top tray was smashed.

"Too bad." Louis poked at the destroyed device with his work boot. "That was probably worth something on the antique market."

"Except it probably belonged to Jack Rabbit Morgan," Ray quipped. "And I'm pretty sure he wouldn't want you to take *it* off the Rabbit River claim, either."

"What makes you say that, Ray?" Wandering over, Alex looked at him curiously. "You don't really think Jack Morgan is responsible for all this stuff, do you?"

"I don't know *what* to think, Alex." Shaking his head, Ray brushed sand and dried leaves out of his hair.

"To be honest, Alex, neither do I." Louis frowned. "I always thought Grandpa was just putting me on, but now . . ."

Alex followed Louis's gaze to the spot where the GET OUT! message had been written in the dirt. The words were gone, erased by the dust devil. And so was any evidence of a flesh-and-blood person brushing out his tracks . . . if there had been evidence to begin with.

"There's no way Matt Montgomery could possibly create a dust devil for his own convenience," Louis said.

"But a ghost could," Nicole whispered nervously.

"And apparently did," Robyn added.

Alex frowned as an uneasy silence settled over the group. Her powers were amazing, but there was a scientific explanation for them. She was sure the same was true for the weird incidents on the desert. Dust devils were common and the appearance of one now was just a coincidence. She also suspected that a clever old man could have rigged the old dry-wash to run and figured out how to escape without being seen. Even so, her normally rational friends seemed eager to believe a dead gold prospector was the culprit.

And why shouldn't they? Squinting against the morning glare, Alex gazed at the endless desert panorama to the north. In a way, the trip to the remote desert had made her feel more like a kid again, rather than an almost-adult. Alex remembered her family vacation last year when she and Ray and her sister, Annie, had to avoid government agents on the trail of a UFO.

Now I'm here without parents on the trail of a ghost, she thought. *What's next year?* She grinned, hoping no one would notice.

Mr. Driscoll seemed to have arrived at the

same conclusion as her friends, Alex realized. He nodded in solemn agreement with the kids' reasoning.

"Well, if old Jack *is* haunting this claim, that's a lucky break for us."

"How do you figure that, Mr. Driscoll?" Robyn asked.

"Simple." Mr. Driscoll grinned. "Jack Morgan's ghost wouldn't be trying to run us off unless there was a heap of gold to find, now, would he?"

"No, I guess not." Louis brightened.

Ray nodded enthusiastically. "That does make a weird kind of sense."

Plunging into the fantasy, Alex added, "But we're not gonna let a few harmless pranks scare us off, are we?"

"I'm *not* scared," Nicole said.

"I am, but"—smiling, Robyn shrugged—"I'm ready for a doughnut."

Sitting on a lawn chair under the tent awning with Robyn and Nicole, Alex swallowed the last bit of her second doughnut and washed it down with OJ. Mr. Driscoll and the boys were huddled around the back of the truck.

"How come boys are totally so enthralled with gizmos and gadgets?" Brushing white powdered sugar off her hands, Robyn picked up her sunblock.

"Don't know." Noticing that Louis had his fingers crossed behind his back, Alex grinned. Mr. Driscoll had just finished setting up his solar power system and was about to plug in a small motor. Obviously, Louis wasn't sure the solar-powered electrical system would work.

Both boys gave Mr. Driscoll their undivided attention as he explained how the system worked.

"It's a pretty basic concept. The photovoltaic panel collects and stores energy from the sun. It's wired to two six-volt batteries, which equal twelve volts. The batteries are connected to an inverter that changes the direct current into a hundred and ten alternating current."

"I didn't understand a word Mr. Driscoll just said." Squeezing a mound of sunblock out of the tube, Robyn spread it over her arm.

"I'm sure there are plenty of girls who like machinery, too." Nicole reached for another doughnut. "I just don't happen to be one of them."

"Neither am I, but I think the point is that Mr. Driscoll can plug in regular stuff and run it." Alex glanced at Nicole. "And an electric motor is quieter and cleaner than a gasoline one."

"Oh, great." Nicole sighed. "Now we can ruin the desert ecology without poisoning the atmosphere or going deaf."

Louis winced as his father plugged the motor into a long electrical cord and flipped a switch. The motor instantly rumbled and purred. "Hey! It works!"

Mr. Driscoll's shoulders sagged with relief. "So far."

"Yo!" Ray called back as he and Louis picked up Mr. Driscoll's wooden dry-wash. "If you guys are done sitting around, we're getting ready to roll!"

"Ready?" Nicole looked from Alex to Robyn.

Rubbing the last traces of SPF-30 sunblock into her arms, Robyn picked up her straw hat. "Hats."

Nicole flipped a white sun visor onto her head with a flourish. Alex pushed on the crown of her bush hat, which she was already wearing. "Hats!"

Rising, the three girls marched to the truck,

where Mr. Driscoll handed them each a pair of canvas work gloves.

"I know they're bulky, but you'll need them. Unless you want blisters, of course." Smiling, Mr. Driscoll tucked a set of hinged metal legs for the dry-wash under his arm.

"No, thanks." Robyn put on the gloves.

Carrying buckets and shovels, the girls followed Mr. Driscoll to a rocky bank where the boys had set down the dry-wash.

"This spot looks like it hasn't been worked much, Dad."

"It's as good a place as any." Sending Louis back to the truck for the motor, Mr. Driscoll attached the metal legs to the back of the dry-wash.

"It looks just like that old one!" Alex exclaimed.

"Sure does, except we won't have aching muscles tonight from working the bellows all day." Noticing Alex's perplexed expression, Mr. Driscoll explained. "The pioneers had to separate the dirt from the ore with forced air from a hand-pumped canvas bag called a bellows."

"We've got an electric motor to shake out the dirt," Louis said dryly. Setting the motor down, he handed his dad the electrical cord. "So we'll just be stiff and sore from digging instead."

Robyn wrinkled her nose. "Why am I not at the mall drooling over stuff I can't afford?"

"You wouldn't have nearly as much to worry about at the mall, Robyn," Ray teased.

"Here we go!" Mr. Driscoll flipped the switch and the electrical motor purred to life. One end of two jointed metal strips was attached to a rod fastened to pulley wheels on the back of the dry-wash under the hopper. The other end was connected to a slanted, ridged tray, which began to move up and down in a jerky motion as the strips pumped.

Whump, whump, whump, whump . . .

"Wahoo!" Thrilled with his success, Mr. Driscoll tossed his baseball cap in the air, then leaped to catch it. "All right! Looks like we're in business."

"Way to go, Dad!" Louis thumped his father on the back.

"Thanks, son." Eyes shining, Mr. Driscoll smacked his hands together. "Now! We'll all run the first load of ore through so everybody can learn the procedure. Then we'll split into two teams. Who wants to dig first?"

Ray immediately volunteered and Mr. Driscoll handed him a shovel. While Ray shoveled dirt and rocks into the top tray, which had a metal screen bottom and was slanted, Louis rolled the large rocks that didn't fall through the mesh onto the ground.

Fascinated by the *whump*ing dry-wash, Alex took in every detail of the ore classification process as Mr. Driscoll explained it.

"The whole system is based on the fact that black sand and gold are heavier than dirt and rock and other metals."

"Black sand?" Nicole asked.

"It's black and heavier than ordinary sand or dirt because of its chemical composition," Mr. Driscoll said. "You can find black sand without finding gold, but you don't find gold without black sand. You'll see. Now—"

Robyn scowled as Louis pushed large rocks off the screen. "Aren't you afraid you're gonna miss a gold nugget?"

"No way!" Louis laughed. "You couldn't possibly miss a gold nugget that size!"

Alex stepped closer. The fine dirt and pebbles that fell through the screen rolled down a slanted, canvas hopper to the ridged tray called the sluice. The sluice angled back underneath the hopper, like >. As the sluice pumped up and down, the lighter pebbles and dirt were bounced down the ridges, off the end of the tray, and into a pile in front of the dry-wash. The worthless dirt and stones were called tailings. According to Mr. Driscoll, the black sand and gold were too heavy to be shaken off and became trapped between the ridges.

Ray paused to catch his breath. "This is hard work. I don't know how long I can keep this up without a break."

"We usually shovel for twenty minutes," Mr. Driscoll said. "That gives us a good batch of con-centrates to pan."

"It's been ten minutes, Ray." Louis reached for the shovel. "Let's switch places for the next ten."

Alex picked up another shovel. "Two shovels will cut it down to five minutes."

"I won't argue with that." Louis grinned.

While Louis and Alex shoveled, Ray rolled the large rocks off the upper screen. Using a small stick, Mr. Driscoll evened out the heavy dirt and pebbles collecting in the sluice ridges. Even though it was still early, the temperature was rocketing into the high nineties and their faces were already streaked with sweat and grime.

"Anyone want something to drink?" Robyn asked. "I feel totally lame just standing around doing nothing."

"Please." Alex had only been working a couple of minutes, but she was feeling the strain. Although she was strong and fit, her muscles weren't used to hard labor.

Mr. Driscoll looked up. "We'll be going back down to the tent in a few minutes, but you could get some ice water ready for the next round of digging. There's a one-gallon thermos jug in the back of the truck."

"Come on," Nicole said. "It'll take two of us to tip one of those large water containers without spilling any."

As the two girls headed back to the tent trailer, Ray called after them. "And don't eat all the doughnuts!"

Determined to hold her own with the boys, Alex drove the shovel into the ground, then tipped it back full of dirt and rocks. Moving one hand closer to the shovel blade for better leverage, she took a deep breath, then heaved the load up and into the screened tray. She struggled to keep pace with the steady rhythm Louis had set.

Dig. Lift. Dump. Dig. Lift. Dump.

"Just a couple more minutes and we'll be ready to move on to phase two," Mr. Driscoll said cheerfully.

"Which," Louis quipped with a smile, "requires some heavy-duty sitting down."

Alex nodded, stifling a groan. Every shovelful of dirt seemed heavier than the one before it.

"Slow down, Alex." Mr. Driscoll frowned. "You'll wear yourself out before noon at the rate you're going."

"I'm fine!" Mustering a smile, Alex hoisted the shovel, but suddenly she didn't have the strength to control it. Instead of dumping the ore in the dry-wash, the shovel followed through the arc of her swing and the dirt landed in a pile behind her. "Oops."

"Don't sweat it, Alex." Louis stopped digging to lean on his shovel handle and wipe his brow. "That happens to me all the time."

Concentrating on the rocks in the screen to make sure nothing golden slipped by, Ray sighed. "It's been over two hours since we saw the dust devil and nothing else weird has happened. Maybe Jack decided to take the day off."

"Probably. There's no reason for him to hang out in the heat." Louis grinned. "Not while he's got us out here doing all the work to find gold for him."

Pausing to catch her breath, Alex started to laugh.

The sound died in her throat when Robyn screamed.

CHAPTER 6

Mr. Driscoll paused just long enough to turn off the motor, then bolted toward the tent behind Ray and Louis.

Dropping her shovel and holding on to her hat, Alex raced after them.

Robyn stood on the truck tailgate scanning the ground as though she expected a zombie hand to burst forth and grab her. Her hat and gloves were lying in the dirt.

"Robyn!" Nicole pleaded. "It was only a spider."

"A spider?" Slumping in breathless relief, Louis shook his head.

"Figures." Ray collapsed on the ground, muttering. "I thought Jack Morgan's ghost was at it again."

"I have an acute dread of anything that walks on eight legs," Robyn said seriously. "I'm allergic to spider bites. Besides, it wasn't *only* a spider. It was a black widow!"

"A big one?" Alex shuddered. Although the distinctive black desert spider was poisonous, the bite wasn't fatal and they didn't go looking for victims.

"Huge!"

Nicole rolled her eyes. "Total leg span about the size of a nickel."

"Where is it now, Nicole?" Mr. Driscoll asked calmly.

"It ran for its life under the trailer when Robyn screamed and almost stomped it to death."

Bending over, Mr. Driscoll peered under the tent. "Don't see it. Guess we're safe." He straightened. "You can get down now, Robyn."

"I don't think so," Robyn countered.

"Come on," Alex coaxed, hiding a trace of annoyance. "You can't spend the whole weekend in the truck."

"Oh, yes, I can." Folding her arms, Robyn stubbornly set her jaw. "I'll itch all over if I get bitten."

"Suit yourself." Nicole waved to Alex. "Help me with the water jug, okay?"

Taking the hint, Alex nodded and smiled. If they couldn't talk Robyn down from the truck, maybe they could embarrass her down by carrying on without her.

Getting a soda from the cooler, Louis popped the top. He took a long swallow, then set it down. "Ray and I will go get the concentrates while you set up the panning gear. Okay, Dad?"

"Sounds like a plan." Moving to the back of the truck, Mr. Driscoll smiled at Robyn. "Excuse me. I need to get that box of equipment behind you."

Setting the large water container upright when the thermos was full, Nicole and Alex watched to see if Robyn would get down. They both sighed as the determined girl pressed against the inside of the cargo compartment and pulled the large box forward. Then she eased around it and shoved it onto the tailgate.

"There you go, Mr. Driscoll."

"Thanks." With a slight shake of his head, Mr. Driscoll carried the box out from under the awning. "Bring that water container over here, would you, girls?"

Alex capped the thermos of ice water and set it aside. Then she helped Nicole drag the heavy bottle over to Mr. Driscoll. Stepping into the sun was like moving from a warm oven into the broiler.

"Wouldn't we be more comfortable in the shade?" Nicole warily eyed a small round three-legged charcoal grill Mr. Driscoll had pulled out of the cardboard box. "Eating cold sandwiches and frozen juice sticks?"

"This isn't for cooking." Mr. Driscoll laughed as he put a green metal pan shaped like a shallow salad bowl into the pan on legs. "It's for panning."

Hoisting the large water container, Mr. Driscoll winked at Nicole. "And the way a gold flake gleams in the sun is a sight you don't want to miss. That's when the fever usually strikes."

"It's not gonna strike me," Nicole mumbled.

Alex peered into the cardboard box. "What's all this stuff for?"

"Get one of those lawn chairs and I'll show

you." Mr. Driscoll filled the legged pan with water. "You can do the honors first, Alex."

Returning with the ridged sluice tray, Ray and Louis carefully set it flat on the ground so none of the dirt and tiny pebbles spilled.

Aware of Robyn's gaze on her back, Alex pulled a chair in front of the legged pan and sat down. Blocking Robyn's view, she hoped to entice her curious friend to come down from her perch.

Alex watched closely as Louis set a plastic kitchen strainer the size of a small saucepan inside the green pan. Then Mr. Driscoll poured the contents of the sluice tray into the water-filled strainer.

"You can do this part, Nicole." Lifting the strainer, Mr. Driscoll waited until all the water and fine dirt had drained out. Then he handed it to the reluctant girl. "Sift through these pebbles. If you see anything that sparkles, holler!"

"Sure." Taking the strainer, Nicole poked through the pebbles with her finger.

Smiling, Alex turned her attention to Mr. Driscoll as he settled onto a canvas camp stool. Ray knelt on the ground between them and Louis watched over his father's shoulder. Picking up the green pan, Mr. Driscoll began to slosh the dirty water around inside it.

Ray started as the man poured dirt and water off one edge into the water in the legged pan. "Aren't you afraid you'll lose the gold?"

"Nope." Louis leaned closer as his father tipped the pan so the remaining dirt slid back into the bottom. "See those indentations?"

Ray and Alex nodded as Mr. Driscoll sloshed, then poured more water off. Black sand and some dirt collected in the long, quarter-inch-deep grooves molded into one side of the pan. Grit and water washed over the grooves and out into the legged pan, where the dirt settled to the bottom.

"The lighter dirt and stuff sloshes out before the black sand and whatever gold is in it," Louis explained. "But you have to be careful not to slosh too much."

"That's right." Scooping more water into the green pan, Mr. Driscoll handed it to Alex. "Give it a shot."

Nervously clutching the pan with both hands, Alex stammered, "Wh-what if I goof and dump it all?"

"Not a problem." Louis slapped his dad's

back. "That's why my dad rigged up the pan with legs. It will catch whatever we dump so nothing's lost. We pan the dirt again to find any gold that accidentally got sloshed off."

"So relax and take your time, Alex. You'll get the hang of it," Mr. Driscoll added.

Breathing deeply, Alex gently swirled the water around the pan. She could see the heavier concentrates collecting in the grooves and poured off a bit of the water. Gathering her courage, she sloshed again and poured. Less dirt and more pure black sand remained in the grooves. As she dipped the pan to scoop more water, Nicole squealed.

"Eureka!"

Holding the green pan steady, Alex turned to look.

"Did you find something?" Robyn called from the truck.

Eyes shining with excitement, Nicole grinned and opened her hand. A gold nugget the size of a pencil eraser gleamed against her palm. "Is this what I think it is?"

"It sure is." Louis nodded, then pointed at Alex's pan. "And so is that."

The threat of a black widow spider attack forgotten, Robyn jumped off the tailgate and ran over.

Alex inhaled sharply as she looked down. Several tiny bits of yellow sparkled in the black sand.

Gold!

CHAPTER 7

"Wahoo!" Leaping to his feet, Ray laughed.
"Gold!"

"Yep." Louis heaved a satisfied sigh.

"Can I see the rest of those stones?" Robyn
nudged Nicole, who handed her the strainer
without shifting her gaze from the nugget in her
hand. Robyn immediately began to pick through
the pebbles.

Alex muffled a giggle as Robyn lowered herself to the ground without checking for spiders.
Gold fever was apparently a highly effective cure
for an acute dread of anything that walks on
eight legs.

Mr. Driscoll fished a small glass jar from the cardboard box. Although any gold found on the claim legally belonged to him, he was letting them keep anything they found. After scribbling Nicole's name on a narrow label just below the black cap, he handed it to her. The vial was only two inches tall and half an inch in diameter, but the tiny nugget would have been lost in a bigger container.

Holding up the small bottle, Nicole stared at the glittering nugget inside. "It does sparkle in the sun, doesn't it?"

Alex gave the green pan back to Mr. Driscoll. "Would you finish this? I'm so excited I'm afraid I'll lose it all."

"Sure." Mr. Driscoll began to slosh. A gold flake and the bits of gold dust miraculously stayed in the grooves as he washed the black sand away.

"Ray and I are gonna get started on the next batch." Picking up the sluice tray, Louis waved. "You girls are on your own."

"I think we can handle it," Nicole said.

Alex watched them run to the dry-wash, then let her gaze drift back across the desert. Matt

Montgomery was standing on a rise near the drop-off, watching them intently.

"Nothing else in this, I guess." Dropping the strainer, Robyn stood up and dusted herself off as Mr. Driscoll pulled out another glass vial. "We're going to work together and split everything we find, right?"

"Sure," Alex agreed as Mr. Driscoll used a toothpick to remove a wet flake from the pan. Most of the gold bits were no bigger than the tip of a pin, but he carefully placed each one in the vial. "The little stuff I panned doesn't look very impressive next to Nicole's nugget."

"Well, if we dig till we drop, it'll add up. And who knows? Maybe we'll find more nuggets," Robyn added.

"Yeah!" Still flushed with the excitement of her find, Nicole grinned. "So let's get started!"

"I'm ready, but Ray and Louis have already snagged the dry-wash." Robyn gestured toward the rise as the small motor roared to life. The boys began shoveling and rolling worthless rocks off the tray as fast as they could.

"You could prospect while you're waiting," Mr. Driscoll suggested.

"Prospect?" Bewildered, Nicole frowned.

"Out there." Mr. Driscoll waved, indicating the whole claim. "Take those big buckets and a shovel to another spot and dig. You'll have to haul the ore to the dry-wash, but you'll be ready to use it when the boys are done."

"Good idea." Robyn ran under the awning to get her hat and gloves.

Slipping the vial with the nugget into her shirt pocket, Nicole buttoned the flap. "I'm game."

"Just remember where the ore in each bucket came from," Mr. Driscoll advised, giving Alex the vial with the gold dust. "So you know where to dig again if you get lucky."

Pocketing the vial, Alex glanced back toward the rise.

Matt Montgomery was gone.

By early evening everyone was wearing out and slowing down. They had spent the whole day digging, hauling, dumping, sifting, and panning through dozens of buckets of dirt and rock. They hadn't even taken a lunch break, but had just made sandwiches and wolfed them down whenever they were hungry. No one had found another nugget, but the bits of gold dust and small flakes had gradually accumulated. Unlike their depleted energy reserves, enthusiasm levels remained high and they were all determined to work until the light gave out.

Dirty, tired, and sore, Alex sat on a rock above the dry-wash while Ray and Louis continued to dig and classify ore with the machine. Mr. Driscoll had wandered off hours ago to field-test a gadget that was supposed to condense and collect moisture from dry air with a humidity percentage below twenty. A device that could provide water in the hostile climate would be worth a lot to desert dwellers. Louis wasn't worried about him, so Alex decided not to worry either—unless he didn't show up by sundown.

Staring into a large coffee can filled with the pebbles Nicole had already checked for nuggets, Alex idly sifted through them a second time. Too exhausted to lift a finger, she used telekinesis to move the small rocks.

Robyn and Nicole were on their way back from the high western butte with one more bucket of dirt. It was the first place she and the other two girls had tried prospecting that morning. Although everyone had dug in several locations around the claim, the ore taken from the butte dig had always rewarded them with specks of gold dust and some sizable flakes. Even Ray and Louis had started digging there and tomorrow Mr. Driscoll was going to move the dry-wash so they didn't have to lug the heavy buckets.

Excited after finding the nugget, Nicole had joined in with the same enthusiasm as everyone else. However, she and Robyn were just a bit upset because the boys were benefiting from their find. No harsh words had been exchanged because Louis's grandfather *was* the legal owner of the Rabbit River claim. But an uneasy tension had developed as the hours passed, which disturbed Alex. If they weren't careful, gold fever might cause one of them to do or say something everyone would regret. As far as she was concerned, a little bit of gold wasn't worth taking the risk.

Setting the coffee can aside, Alex stood up and took the small vial of gold dust out of her pocket. She walked down the incline as Robyn and Nicole dragged their bucket up the slope. Leaving it with the other buckets they had filled at the butte dig, they sank to the ground by the dry-wash.

"You know, guys, I've been thinking." Alex

yelled to be heard over the motor and the *whump* of the dry-wash.

Ray stopped rolling rocks off the tray and wiped the sweat from his eyes with his hand. "About what?"

"Well, it just seems to me that we'd have more fun if we all worked together and split everything *five* ways."

"How come?" Louis stopped shoveling and turned off the motor so they could talk without shouting.

Puzzled, Ray frowned. "You guys have found just as much as we have, so what's the problem?"

Too breathless to speak, Robyn and Nicole stared at her curiously.

"Yeah?" Louis held his and Ray's small bottle of dust by the one in Alex's hand. "Pretty even, I'd say."

"That's the point. We keep comparing to find out." Alex shrugged. "Like we're in competition or something. I mean, it won't make any difference who has more if we're going to divide it all up evenly in the end. See?"

"Uh . . . yeah." Ray scratched his head and shrugged. "I guess so."

Alex's observation seemed to have a jolting effect on Nicole. She blinked, paused, then nodded. "That's a good idea, Alex. And we'd probably get a lot more done if everyone was concentrating on what they do best, too."

Dropping his shovel, Louis sat down. "Like what?"

"Well, like . . ." Nicole glanced at Robyn. "Robyn is a total whiz at panning."

That's true, Alex thought. Robyn's slosh, pour, and dip technique was smooth and fast. She could also spot the tiniest traces of gold dust and slide the black sand back before the precious bits were washed over the rim of the green pan. As jumpy and intimidated as the girl was about so many other things, she had a remarkably steady hand and nerves of steel when it came to panning gold.

"But you've got the eagle eye when it comes to finding flakes in the strainer, Nicole," Ray said.

Taking off her gloves and shaking the dirt out of them, Robyn grinned. "And Alex has a nose for gold. She picked that spot by the butte we've all been digging in."

"And as much as we hate to admit it," Alex added, shifting her gaze between Louis and Ray, "you two have us beat when it comes to muscle."

Louis shrugged. "Okay, so we're all agreed on a five-way split, right?"

Everyone nodded.

"As long as Jack Rabbit Morgan doesn't have a problem with that," Ray muttered.

"Nothing weird has happened since this morning." Robyn frowned. "So maybe poor old Jack decided to leave us alone. I mean, how much gold can we possibly find in two days?"

"So far, we're doing *really* well. I've spent weekends up here with my grandpa when we didn't find anything. So I'm not gonna let a ghost get the best of me. This is Driscoll territory now." Louis looked at Alex. "Got any ideas on how to split up the work?"

"Tomorrow I think we should just play it by ear. Switching jobs when we get tired and stuff. Right now, though . . ." Alex paused thoughtfully.

Now that the gold fever bomb had been diffused, her mind zeroed in on the other situation that bothered her.

Matt Montgomery.

CHAPTER 8

Since she had first seen Mr. Montgomery and his
KEEP OUT! sign, she'd had the feeling that he
wasn't happy having so many kids digging on
the neighboring claim. His late-night visit was
suspicious, too, especially since Mr. Driscoll had
said the old man didn't usually drop by for ca-
sual visits. There was no doubt he was watching them.

The question was, why?

"Alex?" Ray touched her arm.

"Huh? Oh! Sorry." Alex had everyone's worried attention and made light of her momentary
lapse. "Too much sun, I guess."

"It *was* a scorcher today!" Fanning herself with her hat, Robyn glanced at her arm. "My new sunblock sure works great, though."

"So, Alex?" Louis prompted her. "How should we split up the work?"

"I suppose the best thing to do is have Robyn and Nicole sift and pan the concentrates that are in the dry-wash now. Then you can classify the dirt in the buckets from the butte, Louis."

"Works for me." Stretching his arm, Louis rubbed his shoulder. "What are you and Ray going to do?"

"Prospect." Nodding, Alex stared at the spot where the antique dry-wash had been set up. "I've got a hunch."

"Well, don't dig too much." Rising, Louis removed the sluice tray from the dry-wash and held it out. "We won't have much sunlight left to work in after I classify this next batch."

"A couple of sample buckets. Just to see what we come up with." Alex smiled, keeping the real reason for the prospecting foray to herself.

"Your dad's been gone an awfully long time." Taking the sluice, Robyn squinted at Louis. "Aren't you worried about him?"

"Not really. He's probably at the Blue Monday

claim hanging out with Jenny and Bart Riley. *And* trying to sell them one of his desert water makers."

Grabbing two empty buckets, Alex handed Ray a shovel and motioned him to follow as she headed toward the drop-off.

"I hope your hunch about this spot is as good as the one about the butte." Resting the shovel on his shoulder, Ray walked beside her. "We've gotten more gold from there than anywhere else. Except for Nicole's nugget. But you know something? Something you can't *ever* tell my dad? I've never had so much fun working so hard before."

"I haven't, either," Alex agreed. "Who'd've thought it would be fun? But about my hunch—"

Smiling wistfully, Ray didn't seem to hear. "I never dreamed I'd ever get a chance to dig for gold. And then to actually find it! It's like living in an old western movie. Or an old horror film, since we've got a ghost, too!"

"Right. Look, Ray. About the ghost—"

"Strange, isn't it? I hadn't believed in ghosts since I was a little kid—not until you met Danielle Atron's dead grandmother that Halloween."

"Me, too. But I'm not so sure that Jack Rabbit Morgan's ghost is real."

"After all the strange stuff that's happened?" Ray raised an eyebrow. "I think it's all too weird for Jack's ghost *not* to be real."

Alex sighed. "I suppose."

She didn't have the heart to tell Ray that she expected to have the mystery of the ghostly pranks solved before the sun set. In fact, everyone's reaction to Jack Rabbit Morgan's ghost was stranger than the pranks. Although the ghost seemed determined to chase them off the claim, which made everyone nervous and a little scared, they were also thrilled by the idea that the Rabbit River claim was haunted. Even Mr. Driscoll and Louis, who had never quite believed Ben Driscoll's stories, really didn't want anyone to *prove* that the ghost of Jack Rabbit Morgan was just a legend. It was something they wanted to hang on to.

Pausing on the ridge, Alex decided not to worry about spoiling everyone's reasons for believing in the ghost just yet. Her hunch could be wrong.

"We're going to dig here?" Ray stared at the

old broken dry-wash lying on the ground. "Isn't that just asking for more trouble from Jack?"

"*You're* going to dig here, Ray." Alex glanced over the edge of the drop-off. "I'm going down *there.*"

Ray's frown deepened as he peered over the edge. "That's not the Driscolls' property, Alex. We can't dig for gold down there."

Alex just smiled. "I know."

"What gives, Alex?" Ray pressed. "Do you know something I don't?"

"No. Not yet, anyway." Alex looked at him pleadingly. "Just trust me, okay?"

"Okay." Ray nodded, but he didn't look convinced.

Scanning the Amanda Jane, Alex saw the burro munching hay in the shade of the lean-to. Matt Montgomery sat in front of the storage shed, sorting rocks.

To avoid being seen, she squatted behind the rocks and morphed while Ray started to dig. Toes and fingers tingling, she transformed from solid to liquid and glided over the edge of the cliff.

Slithering downward over grit and loose stones, Alex realized the drop-off wasn't as sheer as it looked from above. The surface was covered with protruding rocks and recesses that could be used as hand- and footholds for someone climbing up or scrambling down. *Hmm . . .* she thought, flowing over these spots. However, the real evidence to support her theory was at the base of the cliff.

Pooling in a depression behind a big tailings pile, Alex checked on Matt. He was still sitting by the shed, watching Ray. Alex turned her attention to the cliff.

A large hole measuring three feet wide and five feet high had been dug into the side of the steep drop-off.

Gliding closer, Alex saw that the hole was roughly two feet deep. An ordinary fireplace bellows was lying on the ground inside it. The bellows whuffed as she slid over the handles, pushing them together.

Mystery solved, Alex thought with mixed feelings of delight and disappointment.

Since the old man knew his way around the claims in the dark, he could have released the awning braces and loosened the cap on the water container without being heard or seen the night before. After Mr. Montgomery had doubled back, he had deliberately made noise when he approached the camp so they wouldn't suspect he had already been there.

There were no footprints around the old dry-wash because Mr. Montgomery had erased them after he stood the machine upright. *Probably with a branch*, Alex thought as she reconstructed the scene. Braced against the side of the cliff using the footholds, he had squeezed the fireplace bellows to make the whuffing sound. Once she, Mr. Driscoll, and the other kids had started toward the cliff to investigate, the old man had had plenty of time to climb down and duck into the hole to hide.

There was no doubt in Alex's mind that Matt Montgomery was responsible for the incidents everyone wanted to blame on Jack Rabbit Morgan's ghost.

But why was he trying to scare them? Unless . . .

The opening of the hole was on the Amanda Jane, but what if the interior where the old man was digging was actually part of the Rabbit River?

"Claim jumper?" Alex gurgled aloud, then gasped as a blast of icy air whooshed around her.

Yesssssss. . . .

CHAPTER 9

By the time Alex slithered back to the top of the cliff, she wasn't positive she had really heard the whispered word she thought she had.

Although she wanted to believe in the ghost like everyone else, she had hard evidence that denied his existence. Besides, she knew all too well that apparently impossible things—like being able to shoot electricity out of her fingers or move things with her thoughts or turn into a liquid—usually had rational explanations. In her case it was GC-161. The ghostly activities could be accounted for by the old man's sneaky expertise, knowledge of the terrain, and an ordinary fireplace bellows.

Gliding behind the rocks out of Mr. Montgomery's line of sight, Alex rematerialized and joined Ray. The sun was quickly disappearing behind the high western butte.

"So—what's down there?"

Alex hesitated. Although she knew she could trust Ray to keep a secret, she didn't want to spoil the rest of the weekend by exposing Matt Montgomery or debunking the ghost.

Not yet anyway.

Although the pranks were mysterious and spooky, the old man hadn't done anything to harm anyone.

"Rocks and dirt." Shrugging sheepishly, Alex glanced at the old man. He was still watching them.

Maybe she should tell Mr. Driscoll.

Except she couldn't accuse Mr. Montgomery of being a thief because she didn't know if the hole in the side of the cliff encroached on the Driscolls' property or not.

"It's getting dark. We'd better get back." Handing Alex the shovel, Ray picked up the buckets. "What were you looking for anyway?"

"Doesn't really matter, I guess." That wasn't exactly a lie. Alex intended to tell Louis's dad that the old man *might* be processing Driscoll ore, but not until tomorrow afternoon. It would only take a couple minutes to see if the hole crossed the boundary, so there was no need to rush. Besides, if the hole *was* on the Rabbit River claim as she suspected, accusing the old man of claim jumping would be an uncomfortable experience for Mr. Driscoll. It really wasn't necessary to ruin most of his weekend, too.

But maybe she could stop the old man from bothering them again.

Taking the shovel back to the tent, Alex helped Robyn and Nicole gather firewood while Ray and Louis classified the two buckets of dirt taken from the ridge. When the wood was stacked, they washed up in the water basin sitting on a wooden stand under the awning. Then they changed into clean clothes and turned their attention to dinner.

After arranging hot dogs, condiments, rolls, chips, and the rest of the potato salad on the truck tailgate, the girls were ready to eat when the boys returned with the tray of concentrates. Carrying a kerosene lantern he had borrowed from Bart Riley, Mr. Driscoll arrived just as Ray lit the campfire.

"Where's the water-making thing?" Louis asked.

Mr. Driscoll beamed proudly. "Bart's gonna field test it for me."

"You gave it to him?"

"Right. To test out here on the desert." Totally pleased, Mr. Driscoll jammed a hot dog onto a stick and pulled a chair up to the fire.

Everyone was so hungry, no one mumbled more than a few words until their growling stomachs were satisfied. Ray even topped his previous night's hot dog consumption by one.

"Four hot dogs." Robyn looked at Ray askance. "That's got to be some kind of record."

"Nope." Louis grinned. "My grandpa ate six once."

"I thought I'd be sick of hot dogs after eating them two nights in a row." Warmed by the crackling fire and stuffed, Alex heaved a contented sigh. The rustlings and chirps of desert wildlife played in the background like soothing music and the scent of wood smoke and freshly dug dirt perfumed the crisp night air. "But I think they actually tasted better tonight."

"Because you worked so hard today." Mr. Driscoll winked at the kids.

"My whole body is one huge ache." Groaning, Ray stretched and winced.

"But like my grandpa always said . . ." Louis wrinkled his brow as he shifted into his grandfather voice, " 'Diggin' for gold toughens the flab, fuels the heart, and eases a weary mind like nothin' else—' "

" '—knooown to man!' " Everyone chimed in, then laughed, except Nicole.

"And he was right." Ray swung his arm in a circle to work out a kink in the muscle.

"Yep!" Robyn raised her soda can in a salute.

Mr. Driscoll frowned. "You're awfully quiet, Nicole. Too excited to eat, or just tired?"

Alex frowned, wondering what was wrong, too. Nicole had hardly eaten anything. She had just stared at the fire, her mouth set in a grim line.

"Neither." Sighing, Nicole pulled the vial with the nugget from her pocket and stared at it. "I just can't believe I got so carried away with finding gold!" She shook her head.

"Gold fever." Louis nodded knowingly.

Everyone shifted uncomfortably with the sudden realization that—despite their earlier scoffing—they had been stricken with the fever.

Alex stared at the fire. From the moment Nicole had found that first nugget, they had been digging, hauling, sifting, and anxiously panning dirt hoping to find more gold. And she had been just as driven as everyone else.

"We all caught the fever, Nicole," Ray said gently.

"I know, but I didn't even *realize* I was a victim until Alex suggested that we split everything five ways."

"The important thing is that we're all still friends in spite of it," Alex said.

"Yes to that!" Finishing off her soda, Robyn tossed the empty can into the recycling bag beside her.

"That's true, but I forgot all about harming the environment while I was digging because I just wanted to find another nugget. It's so . . . greedy!" Sighing, Nicole set the vial on top of the water thermos.

A symbolic gesture of rejection, Alex thought. If Nicole didn't have the nugget, she couldn't be guilty of greed. She admired her friend for having her principles, but Alex could see where sometimes Nicole could think herself into a corner.

"Not really." Absently poking the fire with his hot dog stick, Mr. Driscoll glanced at the distressed girl. "No more greedy than being anxious to open your Christmas presents. I believe the key word here is *find.*"

"What do you mean?" Nicole frowned, puzzled.

"You said you got carried away with *finding* gold," Alex said. "Not *having* gold."

"Big difference." Ray's eyes narrowed. "I think."

"Very big difference," Mr. Driscoll agreed. "The excited anticipation you feel Christmas morning is because you don't *know* what's inside the presents. You might really like what you get, but the *thrill* is opening the boxes to find out what you got."

"That's true, isn't it?" Leaning back against a rock, Alex nodded. "Now that I think about it, we were all ecstatic whenever gold showed up in the strainer or the pan, but then we couldn't wait to try again."

"But not just because we wanted to *get* more gold"—Nicole brightened suddenly—"but because looking for it and not knowing if we'd find it was exciting!"

"Exactly." Mr. Driscoll grinned.

"I don't know. . . ." Robyn paused pensively. "I get a thrill every time I put more gold dust in that little tiny bottle. In all honesty, I have to confess that *having* gold is just as exciting as finding it."

"Yep." Ray grinned. "I must have held our vial up twenty times just to see how gold gleams in the sun."

"Well, I'm relieved." Nicole laughed. "Now I can enjoy myself without feeling like I've betrayed my principles. I can deal with being jazzed about *looking* for gold."

"Whatever works." Stretching to relieve the stiffness that was settling into her muscles, Alex yawned.

"And I want to get an early start!" Louis jumped to his feet and began collecting the hot dog sticks.

"I second that motion." Moaning, Ray got up very slowly. "I don't want to waste a minute of daylight."

Gathering the paper plates, Nicole watched Ray hobble to the panning setup with a flashlight. "If you're that stiff now, Ray, you won't be able to move at all tomorrow!" she said with a laugh.

"I'll work the stiffness out. Digging." Shining the light on the ground, Ray looked at Mr. Driscoll. "Should we just leave the concentrates from the ridge buckets in the sluice tray until morning?"

"Probably not a good idea. Someone might stumble over the tray in the dark and spill it. Let's change the panning water and dump them in the strainer."

While Ray and Mr. Driscoll took care of the concentrates, Nicole, Robyn, and Alex picked up the area and put everything away. Louis banked the fire.

"What's that?" Stopping in midstride between the tent and the campfire, Robyn froze.

"What?" Alex closed the cooler lid, then followed Robyn's gaze out across the claim. No moon shone to light up the dark and she couldn't see anything beyond the glow cast by the camp lights.

"I heard someone moaning." Robyn warily backed up.

"Uh-oh." Nicole's eyes widened.

"Moaning like a ghost?" Louis asked casually.

"I don't know." Reaching the comfort of her friends by the tent, Robyn shrugged. "I know it's ridiculous, but I just can't shake the feeling that Jack Rabbit Morgan really *does* roam around this desert at night."

"Yeah, I know." Arching an eyebrow, Louis sighed. "Ever since I started coming out here with my grandpa, I've been hearing about Jack. And even though I know the stories can't be true, there's always this nagging little voice in the back of my mind saying, 'Why not?' Stranger things have happened."

Very true, Alex thought. Her powers were a perfect example of super strange.

"Well, let's assume there really is a ghost. . . ." Robyn paused, then continued when no one argued. "You don't think he'd try to hurt us or anything, do you?"

"He never has," Louis said honestly.

Alex frowned. She was sure the ghost of Jack Rabbit Morgan wouldn't do anything harmful, but suddenly she wasn't so sure about Matt Montgomery.

"I'm not afraid of him." Rinsing his hands in

the washbasin, Ray grinned. "I think he's totally cool."

Nicole nodded. "Yeah. I mean, poor Jack was certainly the underdog. He was robbed and then chased into the desert, where he died. I'm on *his* side."

"Well, I hope he keeps the noise down tonight," Louis quipped as he reached for his sleeping bag. "I just want to get a good night's sleep."

"I'm so tired, I don't think an earthquake could wake me up." Yawning, Nicole turned to go into the tent.

Alex hesitated. She wasn't sure if Matt Montgomery would do more than try to scare them. For safety's sake, she had to tell Mr. Driscoll what she knew right away. But he was moving toward his dry-wash on the slope with a flashlight.

"Ready to go inside?" Robyn looked at Alex.

"Yeah." Shivering, Alex glanced toward the slope as the beam of Mr. Driscoll's flashlight disappeared over the rise. Since it was cold, she decided to wait in the tent.

Still wearing her sweater, Robyn slid into her sleeping bag on the table bunk beside Nicole as

Alex entered. "Zip up the door panel, Alex. It's freezing in here."

"I'm asleep," Nicole mumbled. "I don't feel a thing."

Alex closed the panel, but left the flap over the plastic window pulled back so she could still see out. Then she perched on her bunk to wait.

"Is something wrong?" Robyn asked a few seconds later.

"No. Uh-uh." Alex did not want to trigger any thoughts of impending disaster in Robyn's mind. "Just thinking."

"About what?"

"Uh . . . about, uh, what it must have been like for Jack Morgan living out here a hundred years ago. Before they had trailer tents and sleeping bags."

"Go to bed, Alex." Nicole didn't open her eyes.

Crawling into her sleeping bag, Alex put her head on her pillow.

She didn't remember falling asleep.

Until she was jolted awake when the tent trailer suddenly began shaking and rocking.

Robyn jerked upright. "Earthquake!"

CHAPTER 10

The trailer stopped bouncing as abruptly as it had started.

Robyn and Nicole were unzipping and scrambling through the door panel before Alex untangled herself from her sleeping bag. Outside, someone turned on the camp lights attached to the trailer and under the awning.

Swinging her legs over the edge of the bunk, Alex glanced at the digital clock on the wall. It was four o'clock in the morning. She had no doubt that Mr. Montgomery had shaken the tent. Although she didn't want to burst everyone's belief in the ghost, she didn't have any choice now.

Mr. Montgomery was starting to play rough. Still, she wasn't looking forward to breaking the news. Especially as she listened to the conversation outside the tent.

"That wasn't an earthquake." A nervous tremor infected Ray's voice. "The ground didn't shake."

"But *something* shook the trailer!" Robyn squealed.

"Like Jack Morgan's ghost?" Nicole asked.

"Who else?" Louis sounded upset. "What I don't understand is why Jack's suddenly gotten so mad at us!"

"I haven't a clue, Louis." Mr. Driscoll sighed wearily. "I always thought he liked us."

"Where's Alex?" Ray asked frantically.

"I'll be out in a minute!" Alex called back as she stepped into the doorway.

"Do you really believe in the ghost, Mr. Driscoll?" Nicole asked, surprised.

"Sort of." Mr. Driscoll shrugged. "My dad told me about Jack Rabbit Morgan when I was a kid. When we camped up here and a branch snapped or the wind howled, I was delightfully terrified thinking it was the ghost. I believed it then, and I guess I just never wanted to let go of that particular piece of my childhood. I still don't, but—"

"Uh-oh." Scanning the ground with his flashlight, Louis stopped when the light hit the panning setup.

The pan with legs had been tipped over and the ground around it was damp. The concentrates they had left in the strainer and the green pan were gone.

"Has Jack ever taken anything before?"

"No, Ray." Louis shook his head. "But then, maybe we never found anything *worth* taking before."

Caught in an uncomfortable dilemma, Alex left the tent and stood off to the side while everyone's attention was focused on the dumped pan. She was suddenly very annoyed with Matt Montgomery. Digging into the bluff to mine the Driscolls' ore was pretty low, but destroying the fantasy about a ghost the Driscoll family treasured seemed worse. And the belief in Jack Rabbit Morgan's ghost *would* be destroyed if she told anyone about the hole and the bellows at the base of the cliff.

Robyn edged closer to Mr. Driscoll. "What do you mean, Louis?"

"We've never dug much on the ridge." Louis glanced at his father. "So what if that's where the big deposit is?"

Ray inhaled sharply. "If there is a lot of gold there, we would have found out when we panned the concentrates from the ridge in the morning."

Suddenly everything became crystal clear to Alex. It seemed obvious that the Driscolls had never had any trouble with the old man before, either, or Mr. Driscoll would have mentioned it. More importantly, Mr. Montgomery earned his meager living off his claim. After thirty years, maybe the gold on the Amanda Jane had finally run out and he was digging into the Rabbit River to survive.

"That's possible," Mr. Driscoll said. "But maybe Jack isn't the one who doesn't want us to find out."

"Who else wouldn't?" Nicole frowned.

"It can't be crazy old Matt, Dad." Louis scoffed, then blinked. "Could it?"

"I don't know, Louis. Matt *has* been pressing your grandfather to give up this claim for thirty years." Mr. Driscoll looked toward the Amanda Jane and straightened up. "There's one thing I know, though. I can't put your safety at risk if the old guy is determined to run us off. We're packing up."

"No!" Everyone chorused.

"Nobody's gonna run *me* off our claim, Dad!"

"No way!" Nicole was adamant. "If we leave, whoever is doing this will win!"

"I was just getting used to the ghost," Robyn muttered.

"For all we know, the ghost *might* have done all these things," Ray insisted.

Wrong, Alex thought. If the ghost was real, he *wasn't* responsible for the incidents. Matt Montgomery was. It didn't seem right for Jack to take the blame.

"You can handle old Matt, Dad!" Louis insisted.

"Yes, but I can't protect you from a ghost."

Alex perked up. If she could prove that the ghost meant no harm, Mr. Driscoll might change his mind about leaving.

Then she'd figure out what to do about Mr. Montgomery.

Moving closer, Alex focused on the legged pan. Using her powers so close to her friends made her nervous, but she hoped their willingness to believe in the ghost would avert any questions.

As Alex slowly set the pan upright with a telekinetic thought, Ray snapped his head around looking for her.

Everyone else gasped.

"*That* did not just happen," Louis said flatly.

"Yes, it did." Robyn ducked behind Mr. Driscoll, but she kept her gaze on the pan.

Ray frowned at Alex.

Shaking her head, Alex waved him to look away so no one else would notice her. Then she telekinetically lifted the green pan and put it in the legged pan. She set the strainer back in the green pan.

Everyone, including Mr. Driscoll, just stared in frightened fascination. Ray played along.

"What is going on here?" Nicole whispered.

"There's only one possible explanation." Speaking softly, Ray sighed. "The *ghost* is here."

Enjoying herself now, Alex telekinetically used a hot dog stick to write in the dirt. No one moved. When she was finished, she dropped the stick and eased up behind Ray.

The flashlight shook in Louis's hand as he stumbled toward the spot.

Stunned but curious, Mr. Driscoll checked the pan legs, then walked slowly around the rocks that ringed the still smoldering campfire.

"What does it say?" Robyn grabbed Nicole's arm.

"It says . . ." Louis cleared his throat, "SORRY. STAY."

"Does that mean Jack's sorry he scared us and doesn't want us to leave?" Robyn's voice cracked slightly.

Picking up Alex's writing stick, Mr. Driscoll scratched his head. "Could be. There are no wires hooked to this stuff or anything. But I still don't think staying is a good idea—"

Turning slightly, Alex aimed her electrically charged finger and zapped out the camp light under the awning.

Louis grinned. "Jack doesn't seem to like the idea of us leaving very much."

"So we've *got* to stay," Alex said. Nobody realized it was the only thing she had said since leaving the tent.

"Right," Robyn and Nicole agreed.

"You can't argue with a ghost, Mr. Driscoll," Ray added.

"That's just it, Ray!" Mr. Driscoll looked both

unnerved and awed as he waved the stick. "Unless we're all seeing things, Jack Rabbit Morgan really *is* haunting this claim!"

"Which is totally cool." Louis turned to peer into the dark, looking for the elusive ghost.

Nicole nodded. "And since he *did* apologize, I doubt he'll do anything else to upset us tonight."

"I'm scared of everything, including apologetic ghosts." Robyn shrugged. "But I really want to stay, Mr. Driscoll."

Alex tensed as the man placed his hands on his hips and stared at the ground. She had a plan that might solve the Matt Montgomery problem *and* save Mr. Driscoll from having to accuse the old man of stealing gold and harassing them. If there was a confrontation with Mr. Montgomery, the resulting legal feud with their neighbor would ruin the fun the Driscolls had working their claim. She hoped to avoid that. But if he was determined to leave, she'd have to tell him everything now.

After a long moment, Mr. Driscoll looked up. "All right. But I'm gonna stay awake and keep watch just in case."

"Yes!" Ray cheered.

Louis raised a fist.

Robyn and Nicole slapped a high-five.

Alex relaxed. With Mr. Driscoll standing watch, she didn't have to worry about the old man trying anything else to scare them off before she had a chance to act.

"It won't be dawn for another hour and a half," Mr. Driscoll said. "You kids get some more sleep."

"Great idea." Alex headed toward the tent.

"Did you pick up your nugget, Nicole?" Ray asked.

"No. I left it on the thermos. Why?"

"It's gone," Ray said. "Guess Jack took that, too."

Nicole shrugged. "He can have it."

Grinning, Ray caught up to Alex. "Nice going. I really didn't want to leave. But I have to confess, I'm bummed that there really isn't a ghost."

Alex paused by the tent door flap. "I'm not so sure about that, Ray. *I* didn't collapse the awning last night or run that old dry-wash this morning. And I was sound asleep when the trailer started rocking and rolling."

"Hey!" Ray brightened. "That's right!"

Alex nodded. She had considered telling Ray about her plan, but had decided against it. Everything depended on her powers and there wasn't anything he could do to help. Smiling, she waved as she went inside. ''Night.''

Flopping on her bunk, Alex hoped the others went back to sleep right away. The instant she had seen how quickly Mr. Driscoll and her friends had accepted the existence of a ghost because nothing else explained the moving panning equipment and the writing stick, she had known how to handle Matt Montgomery.

Staring at the night sky through the plastic window, Alex sighed. Although she sympathized with the old man's problem, his pranks and his theft of Driscoll gold had to end.

Alone, she wasn't sure she could stop him.

But Jack Rabbit Morgan could.

CHAPTER 11

Thirty minutes later Alex eased out of her sleeping bag. Tiptoeing to the door panel, she unzipped the lower corner. The night was so quiet, the noise seemed much louder than it probably was, but neither Robyn nor Nicole stirred. She picked up the flashlight she had stashed near the door and tucked it in her jeans. Then, since Mr. Driscoll was on watch, she morphed before going outside.

The warm tingling in her fingers and toes became a pleasant shivering sensation that coursed through her as solid molecules shifted into a liquid state. Dissolving into a pool of ooze, Alex cautiously peeked through the unzipped portion of the panel.

Mr. Driscoll sat in a lawn chair by the truck with his chin resting on his chest, snoring.

The metal zipper teeth tickled as Alex slipped through the panel into the cold, but she didn't giggle. Darkness was essential to success and she had less than an hour before dawn. Dry, broken branches and sharp-edged rocks pressed against the surface tension holding her puddle-self together, but she ignored the discomfort. Racing the sun, she zoomed across the rough ground toward the drop-off.

And slammed into a boulder.

"Oooof!"

Her liquid form condensed with the impact. Squashed and slightly stunned, Alex flowed slowly backward away from the rock. Several seconds passed before she recovered from the unexpected collision. Moving slower, she reached the drop-off and eased over the edge. Her descent ended in front of the hole the old man had dug into the butte.

Spotting the bellows, Alex paused. She only had a vague plan for turning the tables on the old man. The bellows he had used to fake the sound of the old dry-wash might be a very effective prop for convincing him that he had tangled with the wrong ghost.

Sliding over the bellows, Alex morphed it and took it with her as she slithered across the yard. Slipping into the shed under the curled-up corner of a tin panel, she rematerialized and paused to orient herself. Through a crack in the door, she could barely see the stark outline of the trailer in the darkness. No lights shone in the windows.

Flicking on her flashlight, Alex froze when Beatrice stirred in the lean-to on the far side of the wall. Standing still while she waited for the burro to settle down, she beamed the light around the interior. The small shed was cluttered with pans, buckets, hoses, assorted tools, cans, chains and pulleys, bales of hay, and a bag of feed. She almost laughed when the light played across a tier of uneven shelves on the wall by the door.

A vial with a tiny gold nugget was sitting on a tray with several other empty vials. Stepping closer, Alex saw that the label was clearly marked with Nicole's name. Stuffing the vial in her pocket, she turned off the flashlight and carefully opened the door partway.

Rusty hinges creaked and Beatrice snorted.

Alex winced. If the burro sounded the alarm before she was ready, her plan would be ruined.

Taking a chance, she turned the flashlight back on and dumped a scoop of grain into a bucket. Tucking the flashlight and bellows under one arm and carrying the bucket in her free hand, she squeezed through the door.

Snorting, the burro paced back and forth in her makeshift stall and halted abruptly as Alex eased up to the fence. Beatrice wheezed as she inhaled to hee-haw.

"Easy, girl," Alex whispered, gently shaking the bucket. The familiar sound of shifting grain immediately silenced the burro. Shoving the bucket between the slats, Alex set it down and sighed in relief as Beatrice buried her nose in the tasty bribe.

However, a faint glow outlined the eastern horizon. Time was running out.

Stuffing the flashlight in the waistband of her jeans, Alex placed the bellows on the ground and engaged her telekinetic power. The bellows rose and flew to a spot fifteen feet in front of the trailer door. Lowering the bellows to the ground, Alex spotted a broken shovel handle. She telekinetically placed it near the bellows.

The stage was set.

And dawn was no more than fifteen minutes away.

Ducking behind an overturned wheelbarrow for cover, Alex focused on the bellows and telekinetically began to pump the handles together.

Whuff. Whuff. Whuff.

Beatrice's head shot up and she blasted the quiet with a series of startled hee-haws.

The light by the trailer door snapped on and Matt Montgomery flew outside, tucking in his shirttail as he ran. He skidded to a confused halt, then yelped when he saw the bellows. "What the—"

Whuff. Whuff. Whuff.

Mr. Montgomery stared at the bellows in openmouthed astonishment. The handles pumped up and down, but no visible hands were working them.

Alex shifted her thoughts to the broken shovel handle.

The old man took a step forward when the

bellows suddenly fell silent. He jumped back when the shovel handle rose off the ground to hover. Terrified, he turned and ran for the trailer door.

Still holding the shovel handle, Alex quickly erected a force field in front of the door to keep it closed. While the man frantically pushed on the locked door, Alex maneuvered the shovel handle up behind him.

And gently tapped him on the shoulder.

Spinning around, the old man pressed his back against the door. Pale and shaken, he stared at the hovering shovel handle with wide, fearful eyes.

Now that she had his undivided attention, Alex eased the shovel handle back. Even though the old man had tried to scare her, her friends, and Mr. Driscoll off the Rabbit River by playing ghost, she didn't want to frighten him into running away. She just wanted him to do the right thing. Lowering the shovel handle, Alex wrote in the dirt.

CONFESS. JRM

The old man gasped as he read the message,

then nodded vigorously. "Okay, Jack! I will! I promise!"

Dropping the shovel handle, Alex released the force field.

Mr. Montgomery stumbled as the door suddenly opened, but he caught his balance and quickly ducked inside. The first rays of the sun began to lighten the morning sky as he slammed the door closed and locked it.

Beatrice snorted and kicked the empty grain bucket.

Mission accomplished, Alex thought as she morphed. *I hope.*

Using tailing piles and pieces of junk for cover, she glided back to the cliff. She reached the top, just as the orange sun emerged from behind the distant mountains. Pausing behind a pile of rocks, she rematerialized.

Sitting down, Alex leaned against a boulder to catch her breath. Mr. Driscoll was still asleep in the chair and no one else was up and moving about in the camp. And now that the excitement of pretending to be a ghost was over, she suddenly felt very tired.

Closing her eyes, Alex smiled as a cool morning breeze gently blew through her hair.

In a way, she had helped the long-dead prospector keep his word to get any claim jumper on the desert, at least in the case of Matt Montgomery.

But it really was too bad the ghost of Jack Rabbit Morgan wasn't real.

"Pssst!"

CHAPTER 12

Alex gasped and opened her eyes. Shocked by the unexpected sound, she didn't move.

"Alex!" A familiar voice whispered.

Fear and surprise instantly gave way to relieved annoyance. Alex spotted Ray crouched behind the large boulder she had crashed into in the dark. Crawling toward him over the open terrain, she hissed back, "What are you doing here?"

"That's what I was going to ask you."

Safely beyond view from the Amanda Jane, Alex sat cross-legged on the ground and stared at him. Ray stared back, waiting for an answer. Sighing, she explained.

"What a bummer!" Ray sagged when Alex finished.

"Yeah, I know, but I think the old guy is just trying to survive. He hasn't dug on the Rabbit River before."

"That we know of," Ray countered.

"It's been thirty years. Someone would have noticed."

"I guess, but that's not why I'm bummed." Ray shrugged. "Even though you used your powers to make it look like Jack Morgan was in camp last night, I still thought the ghost might be real. It was fun in a creepy kind of way."

Alex nodded, then saw Mr. Driscoll start awake.

"But now that I know Mr. Montgomery was pulling all those tricks, there's no way I can fool myself about the ghost anymore." Ray smiled sadly. "I'm really gonna miss believing in old Jack."

"Me, too. So let's not spoil the fun for everyone else by telling what we know, okay?"

Ray blinked. "I don't want to, but we have to tell Mr. Driscoll that Mr. Montgomery is stealing his gold."

"Maybe not." Alex winked, then waved

toward the campsite as Louis stumbled out of his sleeping bag and headed toward the butte. "Let's wait and see what happens. Jack's ghost might not be real, but Mr. Montgomery doesn't know that!"

"That's right! And he certainly won't suspect that a girl with incredible powers was playing ghost to scare *him*." Ray leaned forward, his eyes twinkling mischievously. "What did you do exactly?"

"Tell you later." Grinning, Alex stood up. "Let's just hope it worked. Come on. We'd better get back before anyone starts asking questions I *don't* want to answer."

Separating, Alex circled around and walked back into camp from the north while Ray strolled in from the direction of the ridge. Fluffing her hair and rubbing her eyes, Alex yawned when Mr. Driscoll greeted her with a cheery smile.

"Looks like you slept well in spite of our ghostly visitor, Alex." Finished spooning coffee into a metal basket, Mr. Driscoll capped it and inserted a metal tube. He dropped the tube and basket into a percolator, snapped the top on, and plugged it into the solar-powered plant.

"Yeah." Nodding, Alex mumbled, "I was so

tired, I just couldn't stay awake worrying about him."

As Mr. Driscoll bent over the cooler to get a jug of OJ, Alex pulled Nicole's nugget vial out of her pocket and set it on the thermos. She put the flashlight by the tent trailer door just as Nicole poked her head out.

"It's morning already?" Bleary-eyed, Nicole groaned as she trudged outside.

Robyn jumped out behind her, looking remarkably awake and alert. "What a beautiful day."

"I hadn't noticed." Ducking under the awning, Louis paused and arched his back. "I'm not awake enough yet to be aware of anything except how sore I am."

Rounding the front of the truck, Ray stopped by the cooler. "What's for breakfast today? I'm starved."

"Doughnuts!" Mr. Driscoll jumped onto the tailgate and crawled inside.

"I thought we ate all the doughnuts yesterday." Unfolding a lawn chair, Alex sat down by the tent trailer where she had a clear view of the ridge.

Backing out of the truck, Mr. Driscoll held up

a white pastry box. "I always stash the supply for the second day."

"Good thinking." Ray nodded. "If we had known, those would have been eaten yesterday, too."

"Exactly." Mr. Driscoll set the box on the tailgate.

Robyn picked up a stack of plastic cups, removed one, then held the package out to Ray. "Well, let's chow down so we can get started. I feel lucky today."

"*You* feel lucky?" Louis asked incredulously.

Unperturbed, Robyn smiled. "How could anyone not feel lucky when the local ghost apologizes and begs you to stay?"

"I suppose." Leaning against the trailer, Nicole sighed. "But I think my luck ran out when Jack took my nugget."

Hiding an amused smile, Alex wondered when someone would notice that the vial with the nugget had been returned. She hadn't even told Ray she had found it.

Holding a glass of OJ and two doughnuts, Louis sat on a rock beside Alex. "Looks like we've got more company."

Alex snapped her attention back to the ridge.

Head hanging and carrying a small bucket, Matt Montgomery was walking toward the camp. Dust billowed around his boots, kicked up by his shuffling step.

Sitting on the chair by the truck, Robyn leaned forward to look toward the ridge as she reached for another doughnut. Ray put one in her hand.

"Hi, there, Matt!" Mr. Driscoll waved.

The old man just kept walking.

"Aren't you usually working at first light?" Mr. Driscoll asked when Mr. Montgomery stopped in front of him.

"Yep."

Ray cast a hopeful glance at Alex. Shrugging slightly, Alex crossed her fingers. Robyn, Nicole, and Louis watched the two men curiously.

Picking up a mug, Mr. Driscoll lifted the percolator and poured. "Would you like a cup of coffee?"

"Nope." Setting the bucket down, the old man removed a leather pouch and held it out. "This is yours."

"Don't think so, Matt." Mr. Driscoll sipped his coffee. "I've never seen it before."

"The gold in here—" Embarrassed, Mr. Montgomery coughed, then stammered, "It—it's from the Rabbit River."

"From *our* claim?" Louis jumped to his feet. His second doughnut fell out of his lap into the dirt.

Alex grabbed his arm. "Let your dad handle it, okay?"

"But . . ." Louis hesitated, then sat back down.

Setting his mug on the tailgate, Mr. Driscoll took the pouch, opened it, and whistled.

Nicole whispered, "What's this all about?"

"Just listen and we'll find out," Alex whispered back.

Robyn nibbled her doughnut, her attention riveted on Mr. Driscoll and Mr. Montgomery.

Smiling, Ray gave Alex a thumbs-up.

Alex shifted uncomfortably. The old man was guilty of theft, but judging from the look on his face, he also felt totally ashamed. But what would become of him if he couldn't dig enough gold to pay his meager expenses?

"All this came from the Rabbit River claim, Matt?" Astonished, Mr. Driscoll peered into the pouch again.

Matt nodded. "I wasn't finding much in my usual spots and dug a 'barrow full from the side of the cliff one day. Found two nuggets and a bunch of dust." Shoving his hands in his pockets, the old man shook his head. "I'm getting old, Big Lou, and it's been getting harder to find enough gold to keep going. So I kept digging into the butte. Twenty feet under the surface of the Rabbit River, but still your claim."

"I see." Mr. Driscoll paused.

"Oh, boy," Nicole muttered.

"To put it mildly," Louis fumed.

Everyone tensed in the awkward silence that followed as the meaning of the old man's words sank in.

"Well, this is great!" Laughing, Mr. Driscoll clamped his hand on the old man's shoulder. "Thanks, Matt!"

" 'Thanks, Matt?' " Ray blinked, totally confused.

"What?" Dazed, Louis stared at his father.

"Huh?" Equally baffled, Mr. Montgomery frowned.

Alex sat up expectantly.

"We hardly ever dig on the ridge, Matt," Mr. Driscoll explained. "If you hadn't stumbled onto this deposit, we might never have found it! We owe you one, neighbor!"

"You do?" Realizing that Mr. Driscoll was letting him off the hook for claim jumping, Mr. Montgomery smiled uncertainly.

"Big-time, Matt. In fact . . ." Mr. Driscoll paused, then handed the pouch back, "consider this your finder's fee."

Stunned, the old man took the pouch. "I, uh . . . I don't know what to say. Uh, thanks."

"You're welcome." Frowning thoughtfully, Mr. Driscoll rubbed his chin. "I don't suppose you'd consider a partnership, would you? A fifty-fifty split on anything in the butte you can reach from the Amanda Jane?"

Yes! Alex grinned.

"Hold it, Dad!" Jumping up again, Louis signaled for a time-out.

"Sit down, Louis," Nicole snapped.

Mr. Driscoll seconded that motion with a sharp look. "How long do you think it would take us to dig down ten to twenty feet to reach that deposit, Louis?"

"Uh . . . good point, Dad." Louis sat.

Alex sighed with satisfaction. Mr. Driscoll didn't really care about the gold. He just wanted to help Mr. Montgomery.

Tugging on his long beard, the old man eyed

Mr. Driscoll warily. "That sounds like a fair deal to me, Big Lou. If you'll put it in writing."

"I will. Before I leave today." Grinning, Mr. Driscoll extended his hand. "But let's shake on it anyway."

Pumping Mr. Driscoll's hand excitedly, Mr. Montgomery laughed. "It's a great dig, Lou. There's no telling what you'll find in those concentrates."

"What concentrates?" Ray asked.

The old man pointed to the bucket. "Uh . . . the ones I took last night."

Robyn and Louis were instantly on their feet. They moved closer to the two men with Ray and Nicole. Alex hung back, just in case another ghostly demonstration seemed necessary. If everyone's belief in Jack Rabbit Morgan's ghost was shattered, the old prospector's legacy of spooky fun and mysterious wonder would fade along with his memory. And that just didn't seem fair.

"You took them?" Robyn asked numbly. "We thought that Jack guy's ghost took them."

"No, I did." Mr. Montgomery shrugged sheepishly. "I, uh, shook the tent, too. Trying to scare you off was a rotten thing to do and I'm really sorry."

"So there isn't a real ghost after all." Robyn sagged with disappointment.

"Wait just a minute." Hands on his hips, Ray looked at the old man narrowly. "How'd you make the pan stand up and a stick write in the dirt all by themselves?"

"That's a good question." Louis fixed the old man with a challenging gaze.

"I didn't." Eyes widening, Mr. Montgomery's voice shook. "Old Jack wrote you a message, too? I mean, you saw it?"

Nicole nodded. "At least, we didn't *see* anyone holding the stick."

Cheeks flushed with excitement, Robyn pointed to the two words that were still scrawled in the dirt.

Exhaling, the old man took off his hat and scratched his head. "I never put much stock in those old stories, but there's no doubt in my mind now. Jack Rabbit Morgan's ghost really *is* watching over these claims."

Ray winked at Alex.

Giving him a thumbs-up, Alex relaxed.

"So who took my little bottle with the gold nugget?" Nicole asked.

The old man flinched. "Well, first I did, and then Jack did."

Puzzled, Nicole frowned. "You don't know where it is?"

"Sorry, missy. It was in my shed. And now it's not."

"Isn't that it?" Mr. Driscoll pointed at the thermos.

"Hey!" Smiling, Nicole picked up the vial. Then she frowned again. "Are you saying you took it, Mr. Montgomery, but you didn't bring it back?"

"Yep."

Ray looked at Alex questioningly.

Alex shrugged and shook her head. The unexplained return of the nugget bottle was the only reason Ray had to keep believing in the ghost.

Closing the vial in her fist, Nicole sighed and gazed out across the desert.

"Ready for a cup of coffee now, Matt?"

"Haven't got time for coffee, Lou. There's gold out there!" Mr. Montgomery waved as he headed back to the Amanda Jane. Halfway to the drop-off, he threw his hat in the air and jumped for joy. "Yahoo!"

"Okay!" Robyn barked. "Time to get busy. Like the man said, 'There's gold out there!' "

"I won't argue with that." Louis slung a shovel over his shoulder. "Ray and I will hit the ridge while you guys sort through those concentrates, all right?"

"Works for me." Picking up the old man's bucket, Robyn moved it to the panning setup.

"Guess I'd better move the dry-wash to the ridge, too." Grabbing a doughnut, Mr. Driscoll headed toward the rise.

"Bring a couple more buckets, will you, Alex?" Ray called back over his shoulder.

"Okay!" As Alex started to duck under the awning, Nicole turned toward the high butte that rose above the camp to the west. "Where are you going?"

Nicole held up the vial with the nugget. "One nugget and five kids? We can't divide it and I wouldn't feel right keeping it. So I'm gonna give it back to Jack."

"That's a really good idea."

"Yeah," Robyn agreed. "Then maybe he won't

get upset if we take the little bit of gold dust we found with us."

Nodding her head, Nicole disappeared behind the trailer.

Carrying a bucket in each hand, Alex walked toward the ridge. The heat of the desert day seeped into her pores as the sun steadily climbed in the cloudless sky. The weekend had turned into an adventure none of them would ever forget, but she couldn't help feeling both happy and sad.

She was thrilled everything had worked out so well. Matt Montgomery and Mr. Driscoll were still friends and the old man would be able to support himself digging Driscoll gold. Even better, everyone, including Ray, had evidence that proved the ghost's existence.

She alone knew that only Jack Rabbit Morgan's *story* had endured the passage of time.

But his story had been her inspiration. Because she had acted in his name, peace and harmony had been restored to the Rabbit River territory. Having to accept that Jack Rabbit Morgan's ghost wasn't real was a small price to pay.

"Thanks, Jack." Smiling, Alex sighed as a cool wind brushed her face.

You're welcome. . . .

Author's Historical Note

The California Gold Rush, which began in 1848 after the discovery of gold at Sutter's Mill, played an important role in settling the American West. Everything Mr. Driscoll told Alex and her friends about the gold rush is factual. In addition, the famine in Ireland and revolutions in Europe drove many people to the United States in search of a better life. Most of these immigrants and the Americans who left homes and families to look for gold did not strike it rich, while many of those who provided them with gear, supplies, and transportation became wealthy. People who failed to find gold decided to farm or opened businesses, beginning a developmental boom in California that continued long after the gold rush ended.

Mr. Driscoll's dry-wash method of separating gold from dirt is also accurate. Pioneers used equipment with hand-pumped bellows, and water was vital to the process and to survival. Under the General Mining Law of 1872, the United States Bureau of Land Management regulates individual claims to mineral rights on federal lands. Some people still live on and work their claims today. There are also panning sites set aside for public use on government land. Several private organizations and clubs offer gold-panning opportunities for the hobbyist.

About the Author

Diana G. Gallagher lives in Minnesota with her husband, Marty Burke, three dogs, three cats, a cranky parrot, and a guinea pig called Red Alert. When she's not writing, she spends her time walking the dogs, puttering in the yard, playing the guitar, and going to garage sales in search of cool stuff for her grandsons, Jonathan, Alan, and Joseph.

A Hugo Award–winning artist, Diana is best known for her series *Woof: The House Dragon*. Dedicated to the development of the solar system's resources, she has contributed to this effort by writing and recording songs that promote and encourage humanity's movement into space. She also loves Irish and American folk music and performs at local coffeehouses and science fiction conventions around the country.

Her first adult novel, *The Alien Dark*, appeared in 1990. She and Marty coauthored *The Chance Factor*, a Starfleet Academy Voyager book. In addition to other Star Trek novels for intermediate readers, Diana has written many books in other series published by Minstrel Books, including *The Secret World Of Alex Mack*, *Are You Afraid Of The Dark?* and *The Mystery Files Of Shelby Woo*. She is currently working on original young adult novels for the Archway Paperback series *Sabrina, the Teenage Witch*.

Sabrina The Teenage Witch™

Salem's Tails™

What's it like to be a powerful warlock, sentenced to one hundred years in a cat's body for trying to take over the world?

Ask Salem.

Read all about Salem's magical adventures in this new series based on the hit ABC-TV show!

#1 CAT TV

By Mark Dubowski

Now available!
Look for a new title every every month

A MINSTREL® BOOK
Published by Pocket Books

2007

Read Books. Earn Points. Get Stuff!

NICKELODEON® and  MINSTREL® BOOKS

Now, when you buy any book with the special Minstrel®
Books/Nickelodeon "Read Books, Earn Points, Get Stuff!"
offer, you will earn points redeemable toward great stuff
from Nickelodeon!

Each book includes a coupon in the back that's worth points.
Simply complete the necessary number of coupons for the
merchandise you want and mail them in. It's that easy!

READ BOOKS, EARN POINTS, GET STUFF

Nickelodeon Magazine.	4 points
Twisted Erasers	4 points
Pea Brainer Pencil	6 points
SlimeWriter Ball Point Pen	8 points
Zzand	10 points
Nick Embroidered Dog Hat	30 points
Nickelodeon T-shirt	30 points
Nick Splat Memo Board	40 points

- Each book is worth points (see individual book for point value)
- Minimum **40** points to redeem for merchandise
- Choose anything from the list above to total at least **40** points.
  Collect as many points as you like, get as much stuff as you like.

What? You want more?!?!
Then Start Over!!!

NICKELODEON/MINSTREL BOOKS POINTS PROGRAM
Official Rules

1. *HOW TO COLLECT POINTS*

Points may be collected by purchasing any book with the special Minstrel®/Nickelodeon "Read Books, Earn Points, Get Stuff!" offer. Only books that bear the burst "Read Books, Earn Points, Get Stuff!" are eligible for the program. Points can be redeemed for merchandise by completing the coupons (found in the back of the books) and mailing with a check or money order in the exact amount to cover postage and handling to Minstrel Books/Nickelodeon Points Program, P.O. Box 7777-G140, Mt. Prospect, IL 60056-7777. Each coupon is worth points. (See individual book for point value.) Copies of coupons are not valid. Simon & Schuster is not responsible for lost, late, illegible, incomplete, stolen, postage-due, or misdirected mail.

2. *40 POINT MINIMUM*

Each redemption request must contain a minimum of 40 points in order to redeem for merchandise.

3. *ELIGIBILITY*

Open to legal residents of the United States (excluding Puerto Rico) and Canada (excluding Quebec) only. Void where taxed, licensed, restricted, or prohibited by law. Redemption requests from groups, clubs, or organizations will not be honored.

4. *DELIVERY*

Allow 6-8 weeks for delivery of merchandise.

5. *MERCHANDISE*

All merchandise is subject to availability and may be replaced with an item of merchandise of equal or greater value at the sole discretion of Simon & Schuster.

6. *ORDER DEADLINE*

All redemption requests must be received by January 31, 1999, or while supplies last. Offer may not be combined with any other promotional offer from Simon & Schuster. Employees and the immediate family members of such employees of Simon & Schuster, its parent company, subsidiaries, divisions and related companies and their respective agencies and agents are ineligible to participate.

COMPLETE THE COUPON AND MAIL TO
NICKELODEON/MINSTREL POINTS PROGRAM
P.O. BOX 7777-G140
MT. PROSPECT, IL 60056-7777

NICKELODEON

MINSTREL® BOOKS

NAME_____

ADDRESS_____

CITY _____ STATE _____ ZIP _____

THIS COUPON WORTH FIVE POINTS
Offer expires January 31, 1999

I have enclosed _____ coupons and a check/money order (in U.S. currency only) made payable to "Nickelodeon/Minstrel Books Points Program" to cover postage and handling.

❑ 40–75 points (+ $3.50 postage and handling)
❑ 80 points or more (+ $5.50 postage and handling)

1464-01(2of2)